AURORA, THE GODDESS OF DAWN, BURNS

JOHNNY GUNN

WOLFPACK
PUBLISHING
— EST 2013 —

Aurora, the Goddess of Dawn, Burns
Johnny Gunn

Paperback Edition
© Copyright 2018 Johnny Gunn

Wolfpack Publishing
6032 Wheat Penny Avenue
Las Vegas, NV 89122

Paperback ISBN: 978-1-64119-437-2
eBook ISBN: 978-1-64119-436-5

Library of Congress Control Number: 2018959660

AURORA, THE GODDESS OF DAWN, BURNS

CHAPTER ONE

"Sun's just about to reach out and grab the sky," Ed Montgomery murmured, nursing his first cup of coffee. His marshal's badge was shined and, as usual, pinned on slightly crooked. There were some who say it represented the man. He was sitting in an ancient cane-back chair on the wooden slats of the walkway in front of his office, the office that proclaimed City Marshal, Aurora, Nevada. "Wish the rest of the day was like this," he muttered. "Hell, wish the rest of my life was this way."

The street in front of the marshal's office was muddy and deeply rutted from heavy ore wagons making their slow way through the crowded mining town. There were rowdy and busy saloons about every other building with hardware stores, clothing stores, and various other shops interspersed. There was gunfire, whoops of joy, cries of pain, and general hullabaloo almost twenty-four hours a day. There was no reason for the sunrise hour to be different, but it seemed to be.

"The way the sun just blasts its way onto this mountain is why we named this old camp Aurora." He sighed. It was a cold morning but no wind and the sun's warmth spread through the man. "Aurora," he said again. "The Goddess of Dawn, how I love thee." Then he had to chuckle to himself and murmured, "I sure as hell ain't no philosophizing old goat of a poet."

If Virginia City were the heart and soul of Nevada then Aurora was the other end. It wasn't a lack of law and order that made Aurora such a dangerous but rich little town; it was the lack of desire for law and order. Those with criminal intent flocked to the mountain city. There were many ways to get rich in a mining camp besides tearing precious metal from rock: Swindles, conspiracy to defraud, outright theft, kidnapping, and high grading are just a few.

The little mining town of Aurora was a roaring camp on the quietest of days, a cataclysmic eruption on a normal day, and according to Marshal Ed Montgomery, there was no such thing as a quiet day. "Well, it's all over now. I had no idea those folks didn't like me, even a little bit."

Every sunrise of everyday for the last three years had found Montgomery in that chair contemplating Sol's arrival with a cup of boiling coffee, strong enough to cure whatever ailed you. "Mornin' Jacob, you're up early," he joshed, as Jacob Swarthmore came down the street with his push broom, cleaning the boards of the walkway. This happened every morning as well.

"Didja see all them riders come in last night, Ed? Must have been five that I counted."

"That be U.S. Marshal Bull Morrison, Swampy. Him and three deputies come to escort that gold to Carson City. Big shipment heading for the mint, but you already know'd that," he chuckled. Ed Montgomery smiled as he got slowly to his feet, grabbed the old chair and took it into his office, plunked it down behind an equally ancient walnut wood desk, and poured a second and last cup of coffee.

Jacob "Swampy" Swarthmore continued down the street, a little tune eking its way out in a hampered whistle. His huge moustache thwarted his efforts. His job was keeping the boardwalk clean every morning, and swamping out three saloons before that chore. If you wanted to know what was going on in Aurora, Esmeralda County seat, you bought Swampy a beer and a shot and listened. Wasn't much he didn't know about the comings and goings in that hells-a-poppin' camp.

The city marshal on the other hand did everything he could to not know what was really going on. "That's why I hired a deputy," he'd say. Montgomery was nearing fifty, ran about thirty pounds or so overweight, and considered moving that beat up old chair in and out of the office as much exercise as he needed. The man was of average height, had brilliant brown eyes, once dark, now snow-white hair, and was generally open and friendly.

"Back in the day," he liked to say, "I had thoughts of making life good and safe for all the good people of the world. I worked as sheriff and town marshal in half a dozen little towns in Texas, and I just never did find any of those so-called good people," his eyes would light up and he'd chuckle some, rip off a chunk of chaw with badly stained teeth, and continue. "Now, I just wait for somebody to do something stupid, which they will, you know, and I have my deputy shoot 'em or jail 'em."

Deputy town marshal was Peter Olsen, just twenty-five but already carrying a sack of history around with him. He killed, not just at the whim of the marshal, but also because he enjoyed watching someone suffer. People didn't use words like psychopath in Aurora, but they should have. No bullet to the head from Olsen, no siree. He'd shoot you in the knee first, then put one in your gut to prolong old man death. Pete Olsen's first two wives died under questionable circumstances, and Marsha, wife number three allegedly left town a year ago. At least no one's seen her.

Conrad Wilson came barging into the office, interrupting Montgomery's contemplation. "Thought you'd have packed it in by now, Ed. Take that badge off and get out of my chair. In fact, you fat bastard, get out of my office." Wilson won the town election the day before by an overwhelming majority and his swagger on this bright morning was majestic despite his lack of size. What he had was presence. What he lacked was tact.

Wilson was a born politician, could glad-hand anyone into believing just about anything. In a mining community where stock was bought and sold on pure conjecture, a man who could persuade was already considered a source of profound information.

What the general population didn't take into consideration, due to their dislike of old Ed, was that Wilson had never worn a badge. He was looking to use the marshal's office as a stepping-stone to better things down the line. Prior to the election he had a long talk with Pete Olsen about how he wanted the office run.

"Yes sir, Pete, I'll just be a figure head, a glad hander. I always have liked the word Senator." He chuckled and sat back in his chair. "You keep the law and order, I'll keep the good times rolling. If I do end up in Carson City, well, son, you just plan on coming right along with me."

Olsen was far more criminal than lawman and considered this the opportunity of a lifetime. No, not the Carson City crap. He had no intentions of working for a senator or governor. Nope, it was gold, silver, and extraordinary power that awaited the young man with a badge. Olsen was built like most people picture Vikings. About five feet eleven, well over two hundred pounds, and just as strong as he looked. Wide heavy shoulders with a massive chest, narrow hips, and long legs made the man physically impressive and dangerous.

"A lot of gold flows down these streets and I plan to have more than my share," he told himself when the new marshal asked him to stay on as chief deputy.

How DOES a man that young get a reputation of bad man or killer? For some, it's just talk. For Olsen it was a combination of talk and deed. There were some who would tell you he killed a sheriff in New Mexico, but no one's ever seen a broadsheet with his picture on it demanding he be brought in dead or alive. On the other hand, when Tea-Bob Taylor called him a cheat at the faro table at the Occidental Saloon last week, Olsen sent him to the great unknown without blinking.

Then there were the stories of those wives who kept coming up dead or missing. Maybe that reputation belonged securely fastened to the big dumb jerk. In his mind, everything he did was meant to be seen and appreciated by those around at the time, and all of that reputation was designed to become legal tender down the line. Gold and silver are the only things that had any meaning to Pete Olsen.

Aurora was three day's hard ride south of Nevada's capitol, Carson City, and was in the news not too long ago about something other than murder and mayhem. Nobody knew where it was. Oh they could get there, but then they didn't know where they were. It seems that town was right on the border of Nevada and California, and was a county seat of a California county and the county seat of a Nevada county. Both states claimed it and there was an almost peaceful settlement of the issue.

Seems as though there was so much crime and bad behavior that California finally said, "Okay, fine, Nevada, Aurora is all yours," and then it had a post office proclaiming it as Aurora, Nevada. Even Mark Twain, up there in Virginia City, had a hard time writing nice things about the old town, and he did visit more than once. Marshal Montgomery thought about asking him to leave town more than once.

Mark Twain's first visit to the area was when he was still known as Sam Clemens and he and a partner had a good claim, visible gold, but hadn't filed the papers yet. His partner was called away on an emergency and figured old Sam would take care of the filing. Clemens was stuck at a place called Nine Mile and figured his partner would file the papers. Sam Clemens lost his claim, started writing about his adventures and those of others, and moved to Virginia City as Mark Twain.

"Nice talking to you, Wilson," Montgomery said,

slapping the badge on the desk. He walked to the stove and picked up the coffee pot and started for the door.

"Where you goin' with that?" Conrad Wilson snapped. The new town marshal jumped up quickly.

"Takin' it home, Conrad. It's mine."

CHAPTER TWO

U.S. Marshal Bull Morrison and Deputy U.S. Marshal Slim Calhoun walked into the Borealis Saloon, got a couple of schooners of cold beer and joined deputies Jory Anderson and Charley Green at a table. "Heard more stories about this town than any other in the west," Morrison said. "We'll meet with Ted Hickson at the express office at three. You get the rooms for us, Anderson?"

Bull Morrison was short, stocky, and mean as cat shit according to many men in Huntsville and other prisons. He carried a knife scar that spread across his face from hairline to lower lip, had fierce brown eyes, wore his black hair much shorter than currently in style. Underneath all that was a sense of humor that some found offensive or at the least untimely. Bull Morrison found it much more satisfactory to beat a man to a pulp in a fistfight than to simply shoot him.

"Room's are taken care of, Bull. Adjoining rooms on the second floor facing the main street. Clerk spent most of his youth sucking lemons, I think." That brought some chuckles around the table. "He's got no personality and won't even say hello."

"We'll shoot him on the way out of town," Morrison chuckled. "We've been here since late last night and seen two men shot down, watched three big brawls right in the street, and haven't seen a single man wearin' a badge. Getting' that load of gold out of town might be a bigger chore than we thought."

"If there's any town left," Slim Calhoun said. "That wire from Hickson sure sounded dangerous. Town people seem ready to burn the place down." He rocked back in his chair and motioned for the barman to bring another round of cold beer.

"Calhoun, I want you to move around town and talk to some of the storekeepers. After sleeping in the straw at the livery last night, it'll do you good. If something's being planned somebody just might say something. There ain't many ranches in this high country, so most of these men must be miners. Meet us at the express office at three."

"Most of these miners you're talking about look more like Texas gunmen, Bull. I'm gonna talk to that smithy at the stables, too. He looked like a good sort."

"WELL NOW, THIS IS A NICE SURPRISE." Slim

Calhoun stepped into the Lucky Lady Café. There was a large sign proclaiming, 'Food Even Better Than Your Mama's'. Calhoun stood six feet and two inches, weighed around two hundred pounds of solid muscle, had broad shoulders and deep chest, and his long arms were as fast as summer lightning when he was pulling heavy iron.

He was one of those few who never aimed his pistol. He just pulled it and fired as a natural reflex. "Hell, boy, pull your hand up and point your finger. It's the same thing. If you take the time to think about it you'll look like a sieve."

Calhoun had a dark complexion, one might call it swarthy even, and wore his black curly hair long. Many thought he was from somewhere in the south when they heard him speaking but he never spoke of family or his past. He was a laid back gentleman, slow to anger, but a maniac when pushed over his limit. His eyes usually sparkled, his smile usually broad and open, and he was usually found with a lovely lady in the evening hours.

"Howdy stranger, grab a seat anywhere that's empty," a soft southern voice called out from somewhere in the back of the building. "I gotta stir the stew and I'll be right with y'awl."

"Yes, ma'am," Calhoun said in a soft drawl of his own. The deputy marshal came into the service after serving two terms as a county sheriff in Missouri, building a reputation of being quite able to bring in his man, dead or alive. He was seriously wounded and then decorated as one of the finest Union spies during the War Between the States. He carried a price tag of ten thousand Yankee dollars issued by General Lee himself.

That's what led to his joining the marshal service.

"Something smells mighty fine back thata way."

The Lucky Lady Café was bright with color and from sunlight streaming through wide windows facing onto the main street. Yellows and greens, reds and oranges, from paint and curtains, filled the dining room with warmth and Calhoun found a table that looked out onto the town. In just moments Angela Whitaker dashed out of the kitchen.

"Well, my goodness, looky here. Ain't you one big boy."

"Hello," Slim said. "Are you the Lucky Lady herself?"

"We'll just have to wait and see," she said, fluttering her eyes some, giving off a beautiful smile. Angela was tiny in every respect. She almost stood five feet if she stretched some, had slim hips, well developed top-side, an oval face that featured a natural smile and bright eyes. Her dark hair was tied up in a bun. She enjoyed being a flirt and was seen in the company of many of the town's more affluent men.

"Don't think I've seen you around. My friends call me Angie. Venison stew is boiling away, or you can pick from the menu." She pointed at a chalkboard hanging on the wall near the kitchen door. "I try to open about sunrise and close this place down late in the afternoon. You're new here."

He was taken by her open friendliness, her provocative flirting, and her charming good looks, and decided to be just as forward as she had been. "My first choice for something in the cafe would be Angie," he smiled. "I guess I better stick with the venison stew." He was looking straight into her deep blue eyes when he said it and gave her a little wink.

She didn't blush or turn away, just looked back into his dark brown eyes and smiled brightly. "One bowl of venison stew comin up, sweetie. Coffee pot's on the big stove back there. Grab some while I get your dinner." He watched her narrow hips sway gently as she almost strolled into the kitchen.

Calhoun was pouring coffee when Pete Olsen came in and he nodded to the big man. He was settling into his chair and heard Angie call out a welcome to the new customer.

"Be right with ya, Pete, honey. Old Hickory Smith shot himself a big old deer yesterday so I got some good venison stew boilin' away in here. Wantcha self some?"

"Yeah, and make it snappy," Olsen growled slipping out of his heavy wool coat. "I ain't got time for talking nonsense, woman."

Calhoun spotted the badge immediately and wondered just what kind of a man this deputy was to talk to someone as nice as Angela Whitaker that way.

"That stew does smell good, ma'am," he said. He and Bull Morrison had decided that until it was time to escort the gold shipment the deputies wouldn't wear their badges. If there was some kind of trouble brewing they might find out about it if it weren't known who they were.

Angie came out of the kitchen with a large bowl of stew in one hand and a platter of sourdough biscuits in the other. "I'll getcha a tub of butter and jam in a second, mister. Hey!" She yowled, "You haven't told me your name yet. That ain't fair, buster. I told you mine." She was laughing and almost dancing around some.

"Yes, you did, Angie." He jumped to his feet. "My friends call me Slim. Slim Calhoun at your service, ma'am." He gave her a big smile and got one back along with a wink. He wanted to just gather her up and hold her tight. "My heavens, I've lost my manners."

"Come on, Angie, dammit. I ain't got time for all this crap. I got a meeting with Silas and I'm hungry. Quit carrying on and get my food."

"Easy, mister," Calhoun said. "The lady's just being nice to a customer."

"You talkin' to me? I ain't a mister. I'm Deputy Town Marshal Pete Olsen, stranger. You call me Deputy Marshal Olsen or you don't talk to me." He was half way out of his chair as he was spoutin' off.

Calhoun chuckled some, nodded to Angie, and turned to Olsen. "Yup, I was talkin' to you, mister. Got yourself riled some, eh? Well, settle down and you won't get yourself hurt none." He took half a step toward the deputy, still wearing a smile.

Olsen flung his chair back jumping to his feet. "You don't talk to me that way, saddle tramp. You stand back, mister, and I mean now. Nobody threatens the law in this town." His right hand was hovering close to the Colt he carried, his eyes were blazing with hate and anger, and his legs were slightly spread for balance.

"You got yourself all riled, son." Slim Calhoun set his legs and arms for a killing but instead picked up a clean napkin and wiped his mouth and slowly stepped from the table. "Don't know what's in your craw, but you damn well picked the wrong man to get riled up about. I'm gonna reach in my shirt pocket and show you something, so just quiet yourself down some."

right hand hovered very near his heavy Army Colt while he reached into his shirt pocket with his left. His eyes were narrowed to slits and anyone with the least awareness would have seen death in his face.

Olsen's hand actually gripped the handle of his sidearm as Calhoun pulled his vest to the side and pulled his badge out. In large print it read, Deputy U.S. Marshal. "Name's Deputy U.S. Marshal Slim Calhoun, mister. Now, sit yourself back down and behave. You're in public now, not at a pig sty."

He put the badge back in his pocket and stared at Olsen with just the hint of a smile on his broad face. The deputy town marshal didn't say anything. He spun and stomped out of the café, slamming the door hard enough to rattle tableware on the shelves. "Some men just shouldn't carry a badge, Angie. Sorry you had to see that."

"A U.S. Marshal? Well, now, I'll just be danged at that. Now, my new friend, you straightened that young Olsen right out. That venison stew is on the house Marshal."

"A real man would never speak that way to a lady. Just call me Slim." She thought she'd never seen a more delightful smile on a man, her knees were just a bit on failure side, and was ready for this tall stranger to wrap her up and cart her off.

SILAS HOUSTON WAS behind the counter at his feed, farm, and ranch supply store discussing the ins and outs of properly feeding goats when Olsen stormed in. Houston was a beefy man, not particularly well proportioned but strong as any ox in the territory. Along with his feed and supply business he also provided mining equipment for some of the high graders in the area. Barrels of black powder, fusing, blasting caps, picks and shovels adorned an entire section of his large mercantile building.

"Morning Pete. Got the new marshal all settled in?"

"Yeah, Wilson's sittin' in that damned old chair the same way old Ed did. We got us a little problem, Houston. There's a deputy marshal, U.S. Marshal, in town He just might gum up the works. I almost shot him before he showed me his badge. Shoulda."

"Damn, damn, damn," Houston said. He was pacing back and forth behind the counter, wagging his head about. "Does Harrison know about this? That shipment's leaving early tomorrow morning according to Brady."

"You talked to Brady?" Olsen smiled just a bit. It was an ugly smile as he remembered beating Brady Throckmorton to a bloody pulp just a week ago when the man wouldn't tell him about the gold shipment. Throckmorton was the assistant manager of the Sierra Express Company office in Aurora.

"He's looking to kill you, Pete, and he'll do it the same way all cowards do, from the back. He said armed guards would escort the gold out tomorrow morning at about four or so. He didn't say nothing about federal marshals. Did you talk to Harrison?"

"No I wanted to tell you first. Last time I talked to Harrison he thought the shipment was to be on Saturday, not Friday. What else did Brady tell you?"

"Let's go see Harrison and get this figured out. We need to move fast if that shipment's leaving in the morning. Damn, damn, damn." Silas Houston came around the counter slipping into a heavy coat. "Harrison ain't gonna like this but it ain't his call, either." He turned to a man standing near the door. "Take care of the place, Johnny. I'll be right back." The two men stepped out onto the loading dock to head to Harrison's mine office.

"It's just like him to make these kinds of plans, to do what we want to do on Saturday morning without knowing that we have to do it on Friday morning. Man just gets all wrapped up in hisself and don't pay no attention to the facts of the matter."

Olsen and Houston walked down off the loading dock to walk the short block to the mine office where they hoped Wendell Harrison would be. "There he is," Olsen said. He was pointing at a tall man striding down the boardwalk toward the blacksmith's barns. "That's the marshal. Looks to be alone, so he won't be much of a bother. I can take him in a minute.

"Those people are always so proud of themselves, always U.S. Marshal, not just marshal, and puffing up some. I'll take the wind out of his sails, Silas."

"Don't get riled, Pete. It's far more important to get the gold than it is to get in a fight with a marshal. According to what Harrison said, this is a shipment of gold bars from three of the mines. You can bet most will be from the Del Monte. We got to know what Harrison's plans are and make the changes so we can hit them in the morning. Don't lose your target, Pete. It's gold, not a marshal that pissed you off."

CHAPTER THREE

———

"Good morning to you," Slim Calhoun said. He walked into the blacksmith's open-air set up next to one of his barns. "Thanks for letting us catch some winks after our ride in last night. We'll be at the hotel tonight."

"Yeah, one of the boys came and got your gear just a while ago." Angus McMurray's shoulders were almost as wide as the barn doors, his wild red hair was tied back Indian style with a red bandanna braided into it, and his beard, equally red, equally wild, was thick with coal dust. McMurray's stables cared for the express company animals, had animals to rent, and provided care and feed for travelers. The big man often acted as the town vet, as well as being the best black-smith in the territory.

"That horse of yours is gonna come up lame if you don't get those shoes changed out."

"That's why I'm here, Mr. McMurray. Would you do the honors, sir?"

"Aye Bucko, I'll be glad to and so will your horse. Anything else I can help you with? That heavy-set man you rode in with, Bull Morrison, is a federal marshal? You too? And would you be here for a reason?" He had a little smile showing through his wild moustache and Calhoun swore he gave a bit of a wink. McMurray's eyes did twinkle some and he carried the lines of a warm and happy man creasing his face, the lines running out from the sides of each eye.

"You're a crafty one, McMurray. We're not telling everyone who we are, and we're here to protect a gold shipment that will be coming up. Heard any talk around town about that? Oh, and would you have a pot of coffee boiling away somewhere?"

"Where have I left my manners?" McMurray said and led Calhoun into an office tucked away inside the barn. "Gold shipment, eh? That's why old man Hickson wants a six up rig tomorrow morning. I haven't heard any talk about such a thing, though." Calhoun didn't believe a word of that. McMurray poured two cups and pulled a flask from a desk drawer. "Some sweetener, Marshal? Comes from Kentucky."

Calhoun watched as the blacksmith made their coffee more than sweet and took the offered cup. "Whew, that is sweet," he said. "And good. This does come straight from Kentucky. If someone might be talking about a gold shipment, where would they most likely be?"

"There's fifteen saloons filled twenty four hours a day, Marshal. Pick one and there will be a criminal element at the bar. There are thousands of men in this town looking to get theirs one-way or t'other. Only thing I know is to have a six-up rig ready to roll by four, tomorrow morning."

Calhoun gave his thanks, figured with what that coffee was laced with he better shy away from saloons for the time being. He was headed for the feed and supply store when he bumped into Bull Morrison. "Heard anything, Slim?"

"Hickson ordered a six-up team for tomorrow morning and there's a real piss-ant deputy town marshal that needs to be brought down several pegs. How about you, Bull?"

"I could use a cold beer. Where would you hit the shipment if you were doing the planning?"

"I'll have one with you, but I just had some of the finest bourbon I've tasted since coming west. That blacksmith knows his liquor." They walked into the Occidental and found seats at a table toward the back where the gaming tables were. "I doubt very much that McMurray would be part of a hijack but I wonder who he might have told about what Hickson ordered. It would have an impact on how we will get that load out of town.

"With a six-up rig we'll have to stay on the main

roads. Probably down toward the Walker River and through that canyon." He had a contemplative look that Bull Morrison took in immediately.

"That canyon narrows down quite a bit, crosses and re-crosses the river several times. Wouldn't be hard to force the wagon to a stop. With two of us in front and two behind," and he stopped, took a long breath, and just shook his head. "That load of gold and silver is destined for the Carson Mint, Bull, and would tempt just about anyone." Both men knew there was enough of it that someone riding the outlaw trail could put together a gang to take it.

"Yeah," Bull Morrison said. "We might want to change the plans on Mr. Hickson, go with two teams instead of three, and take the high road out of town. It's rougher, going over Lucky Boy Pass, and longer, but will be a hell of a lot easier to defend."

"That's a high pass, Bull. It's eight thousand feet or more and this time of year, we'd be taking a hell of a chance. Simple thunder storms at five thousand feet are one thing, but they become blizzards way up there." The two were chuckling some but also recognized the danger of the situation.

"Do you have the authority to force Hickson to make those kinds of changes? I heard he's kind of an uptight little snot to deal with."

Morrison blew some foam off a schooner of beer and chuckled. "Yeah, he is that, but I'm working for the United States Mint, which just happens to own the gold we'll be protecting. Yup, my fine friend, we have the authority. Let's not say anything to anyone about this.

"I'll bounce it off Hickson and if he disagrees, we will just go along with him until four tomorrow morning and make the changes at the livery."

"You're a seriously underhanded bastard," Calhoun laughed.

As they were walking out the door a man at the bar slammed into them, cussing a blue streak. "Out of my way, jackass. I'm late for my shift." He took a round-house right toward Bull Morrison's head, which never quite made it. Morrison grabbed the man's fist with both hands and whirled completely around. Everyone in the saloon heard the bones break and tendons tear. The shriek of pain was several decibels less.

Morrison stood with the man dangling from his now useless arm. "Name's Bull, not Jackass. I think you just blew your shift." Morrison stood the man up straight and put a fist straight into his face, splashing the man's nose flat.

"I just never have cottoned to that name Jackass. My name's Bull," he said softly, easing the man gently to the filthy saloon floor. "Bull. Got it?"

"Now there you go, gettin' all riled over some-thing." Calhoun was chuckling right along with Morrison as they stepped onto the boardwalk outside the saloon. "Can't take you anywhere."

"GOOD MORNING, WENDELL," Houston said step-ping into Harrison's office. The Starline Mine and Mill offices were on a side street, which during the early spring and late fall was actually a running stream. Winter found it iced and summer found it muddy. "Olsen just found out there's a U.S. Marshal come to town and Brady told us the shipment schedule, which is not Saturday but tomorrow." Silas Houston got it all out in one breath.

To say Houston was intimidated by the mill foreman would be obvious to anyone, but with Hous-ton's large size it didn't seem right. Wendell Harrison dressed as a well-to-do business man, not a miner, and acted more as a banker than someone dealing with rock and ore. Pete Olsen on the other hand had never felt intimidated by anyone.

"What made you think the shipment was Satur-day? We need to know a hell of lot more about this shipment than you've told us, Harrison." Olsen didn't wait to be invited, and sat down in a wingback near Harrison's imposing desk. "The gold is leaving tomorrow morning, early. We don't know which road will be used, we don't know how many guards will be riding shotgun. We don't know shit," he growled.

"Take it easy, Pete," Harrison said. He was almost fatherly with the young marshal, which infuriated Olsen. "I just got the orders from the mine superinten-dents and from Hickson. The mines will deliver the ingots to McMurray's barn at four, tomorrow morning and they will be carried north by a six-up rig on the Walker River Road. There are supposed to be four, maybe more, U.S. Marshals to ride guard on the shipment.

"We will leave town quietly and not as a group well before that. How many guns have you put together, Houston?"

"Pete and I have five men lined up, all good with guns. With us, that will give us eight guns, which should be more than enough. If they go the main road, we can ambush that wagon somewhere in the Walker River Canyon."

Harrison sat back in his leather chair, lit a cigar, and smiled at the two. "Sounds like we'll be breaking that shipment into shares for us before supper tomorrow night, gentlemen. Any questions?" He sat back with a proud and dignified look on his long face and almost flicked his hand as if saying, "We're through. Go play now."

Olsen had several questions but Houston hustled the two of them out the door and onto the muddy street. "Don't get riled, Pete. I have a plan, too. Let's go have a beer and talk some."

"What kind of a plan?"

"I don't trust Hickson or Wendell, Pete. Wendell is too easy in accepting that there will be a six-up hitch. I think we need to wait until the wagon leaves and follow rather than set up and hope they come that way."

"Old Wendell Harrison ain't gonna like that," Pete Olsen grinned.

MORRISON AND CALHOUN found their way to the Borealis Hotel Saloon for just one more cold beer and got settled at a table. That's when Calhoun spotted Houston and Olsen coming in. "That's the deputy city marshal I was telling you about. I think the man with him is Silas Houston, the feed store operator. Neither man has the best reputation around town."

"That sounded like you're thinking something, Slim."

"Silas Houston has been involved in thefts before and Olsen's got a bad attitude. I haven't heard anything about holding up our shipment, but those two would be capable. Houston supplements his merchandise at the expense of others, I think. Wagon loads of supplies destined for Body or Mono have disappeared and Houston's supplies have increased from time to time." He was chuckling as he told the story.

Olsen saw Calhoun as soon as they stepped in the batwing doors and edged he and Houston toward the bar and away from the tables. "Let's just have a quick shot and get out of here. That's the federal marshal at the table back there."

"You suppose both those men are marshals?" Silas asked. "Don't see no badges on either one. Maybe that big guy was spoofin' you, Pete."

"Nobody spoofs me, Houston," Olsen growled. "He had his tin star in a shirt pocket. I want to talk a lot more about tomorrow but not here. Not with those two sittin' right there."

Houston watched Bull Morrison get up and stroll to the bar. That horrible scar across his face made him look mean and nasty, and the slight grin made it gruesome. Once again Houston found himself intimidated. "How do?" Morrison said stopping in front of the two. "Understand one of you gentlemen is a deputy town marshal. Which one would it be, the old guy or the kid?"

"I ain't no kid, mister. I'm Deputy Marshal Olsen. What's it to you?"

"I appreciate a well mannered boy, I do." Morrison smiled watching Olsen tighten up, gripping the bar so hard his knuckles were white. "What's your name old-timer?" Morrison was aching for a fight and didn't give a damn where it came from.

"I'm Silas Houston, owner of Aurora Feed and Supply." Once again the big man was intimidated and quietly asked, "Who might you be, stranger?" Houston and Morrison were about the same size, both considerably heavier than Olsen, and both in prime physical condition. Houston held out his hand and Morrison felt strong fingers as they shook.

"Nice meeting you, Houston. I'm U.S. Marshal Bull Morrison." He glanced at Pete Olsen, then to Houston, and finally to Calhoun. "That's my deputy

Slim Calhoun at the table. He tells me you're not very friendly, Mr. Olsen. That's a shame, cuz we're always looking to make friends."

"I don't much care for your attitude," Olsen said.

"Too damn bad," Morrison prodded. "I got my attitude cuz I don't much care for ugly little boys hiding behind a badge and being nasty to women."

Olsen slammed his hand down on the bar, rattling glasses and bottles, getting ugly looks from patrons, and a scowl from the barman. "You ain't got no call talking to me like that. How do I know you're really a marshal anyway?"

"Cuz I told you I was." Bull Morrison looked over at Calhoun and cocked his head, inviting the deputy to join the party. Slim downed his beer and slowly got to his feet. He had a smile on his face and was halfway to the bar when Angie Whitaker walked in.

"Well now, ain't this a party I just walked into. Howdy Slim Calhoun," she smiled slipping her arm through his. "I'm hot and tired and need something cold." She and Slim made the last few feet to the bar, Silas Houston moving back some to give them room. "Pete Olsen," she said. "You hanging out with the big boys, eh? Federal marshals, kinda like the top dogs, I guess." She looked at Bull Morrison.

"Somebody sure whupped on you bad. I'm Angie."

"Hello, Angie, I'm Bull." He gestured to the barman to get Angie, he, and Slim beers, leaving Olsen and Houston out. It wasn't often that a woman would be allowed to stand at the bar, but the barman heard the words U.S. Marshal bandied about enough that he wasn't going to say anything.

Bull Morrison touched the scar near his eye. "Man came to a gunfight with a knife is what this is all about," he said, letting his finger lightly follow the big scar.

"There are some real nasty people in this old world of ours," Angie said, and looked right at Pete Olsen. She turned to Slim Calhoun and smiled, "And there are really nice people too if you look around some."

Morrison was frustrated at Angie's coming in knowing that he wouldn't be able to goad Olsen into a fight or worse with her standing right there. "Guess we might as well amble on down the street, Slim. Looks like out party's been cancelled." He turned to Houston and Olsen and tried his best to smile.

"Maybe we'll run into you boys down the line, eh? Mr. Olsen, be careful how you talk to grownups, particularly when they carry heavy badges marked U.S. Marshal. Many aren't as amiable and generous as us two."

Houston was sure Pete Olsen would go for his gun and stepped back, taking Angie with him. The barman slipped his hand under the bar, making sure the double-barreled shotgun was still there, and Slim Calhoun just stood still with a big grin on his face.

"Nice talking to you," Calhoun said, and he and

Bull Morrison turned and started toward the swinging doors.

Olsen bawled "No!" and Bull Morrison spun around, his Colt out and cocked, aimed at Pete Olsen's face. Olsen froze, his hands slowly moving out from his body, his eyes bigger than five dollar gold pieces, and for the first time in his young life felt the ice of fear as it flowed through his veins.

The silence in that old saloon was as heavy as the crushing rods at the Aurora Mill as Morrison slowly dropped his weapon and slipped it back in its leather holster. Eyes still blazing with a desire for blood, Morrison turned his back on the deputy and walked with Calhoun out onto the street.

"That went well," Calhoun joshed as they headed for the Sierra Express Company offices and their meeting with Ted Hickson. "I'm afraid that boy probably didn't learn much from our little encounter."

"You thinking there might have to be another learning session? It's okay by me," Morrison chuckled. "He's got a serious ugly side to him."

Calhoun looked at Morrison and got a big old grin on his face. "I guess you'd know that."

CHAPTER FOUR

IT TOOK SILAS HOUSTON AT LEAST HALF A BOTTLE of rotgut whiskey to calm Pete Olsen down after his brush with Bull Morrison. "You've got to get yourself put together Pete. Let's find our crew and make the plans we know we have to have. Come on, now."

"I'm gonna kill that bastard," is all Olsen said as they walked out to find Jake Jackson and his little gang of gunmen.

"You might want to put that off until we get several hundred pounds of gold in our hands. We're gonna be rich, Pete. Let that point take hold, will you? You're looking to screw me and Harrison out of a lifetime of money cuz you got your feelings hurt. Get it together, Pete. We're runnin' out of time." Houston was holding his anger in check but could feel it building. *Damn marshal was right calling this fool a boy. If I lose this gold because of his stupidity I'll kill him twice.* Houston's thoughts continued in an ugly vein for some time. What he would never be able to reconcile with himself is the fact that somebody like Wendell Harrison could intimidate him with just a look, but he wasn't really afraid of this psychopathic killer.

Houston threw fifty pound bags of feed around like a child's ball, lifted crates of merchandise that weighed more than he did several times a day, yet a man in a starched shirt and waist coat intimidated him. He could pick Harrison up and break him in half anytime he wanted.

They walked into a barn that Silas Houston used as a storage warehouse and found Jake Jackson and four other men waiting for them. "Been a couple of changes since our last meeting, Jake." Houston motioned for everyone to gather around a table near the back wall.

Jackson came to Aurora as a miner for the Del Monte, one of the most productive of the mines, and made good money high-grading ore during his shifts until he got caught. Now he's a two-bit thief under the watchful eyes of Pete Olsen who is teaching him everything he knows.

Local thieves and armed robbers make up the rest. Eddie Payson would probably be considered the meanest of the group, about on a level with Olsen. A fella by the name of Childers had robbed a widow or two of their dead man's pensions, Tiny West was accused of attempted bank robbery, and the only one of the bunch who had served time for an actual crime was Jamey 'Balderdash' Emory.

Emory stopped the Aurora to Body stage, took lots of cash and possessions and came right back to town and got drunk. When something is said that he doesn't understand, or whatever, he comments, loud and furious, "Balderdash."

"I know we talked about this operation of ours being on Saturday, but that timetable has been changed," Houston said. "There are a couple of other changes that we need to make. There are at least two federal marshals in town to escort that wagon load of gold and silver"

"I ain't worried about two marshals," Jake Jackson said "Hell, me and Pete can take care of them." He was a cocky little snipe and idolized Pete Olsen to the point of following him around, walking and talking like him.

"Don't get too sure of yourself about that," Houston said. "I just saw one of them draw down on Pete there, and I've never seen anything that fast."

Not a sound was made as the seven men at the table understood what Houston just said. People didn't draw on Pete Olsen and live to tell about it. Olsen sat at the table, almost shaking with anger, his eyes cutting Houston to ribbons, his knuckles white and ready to kill anything that moved.

"Balderdash," Emory said, breaking the spell. "There's still eight of us if the dandy Mr. Harrison plans to join us."

"The plan right now is for the gold to arrive at McMurray's stables early tomorrow morning and the wagon, pulled by six-up will leave at four o'clock with the marshals guarding." Olsen was spitting the words out, desperately trying to hold his anger in check. "If that's the true plan, they would be forced to go down the main road and connect with the Walker River Road."

"You said if that's the case, Pete. You have doubts?" Tiny West sat forward in his chair wishing someone had brought a bottle. "We could just ride to the canyon and cut 'em off."

"That's what has me bothered," Olsen said. "It's what Harrison told us that he heard from Brady Throckmorton. It's too obvious. With three teams they would almost be forced to go that way, Tiny. Harrison said just what you said about the canyon." Olsen rocked back and forth on the spindly legs of an old cane-back chair, pulled a cigar and got it lit, still thinking.

"Those marshals me and Houston met today would not let that happen. Harrison wants us to ride out well before the wagon and ambush it at the canyon. We'd sure feel pretty damn dumb if the wagon took the other road, eh?" He actually laughed, getting the others to chuckle a bit. "Pretty damn dumb."

"Well, what do we do?" Jake Jackson asked. "Why didn't somebody bring a damn bottle?"

"Childers, go get us a bottle, maybe two. We got

some serious plannin' to do and we don't have a lot of time to do it." Houston handed the man a couple of coins and sent him on his way. "I want the change," he said.

"Balderdash," Emory exploded. "Ain't no plannin'. We just follow those fools out and take the wagon when they get out of town."

"That's pretty close to what I was thinking," Olsen said. "If we are saddled and ready to ride when they pull out we can just follow along, well behind them, whatever road they take. It would be damn obvious though for anyone up and about that time of the morning."

"If we are scattered all over town like we're getting ready to ride somewhere and follow out individually, it wouldn't be obvious," Silas Houston said. "We could meet up down the trail and make our hit."

"Good, Silas," Olsen said. "If they take the mountain road out, where would be the best place to hit that wagon? I've only been on that road once and don't remember much about it."

"I know that road," Tiny West said. "Use it all the time to get meat. Deer run through there thick sometimes. Lucky Boy Pass is the perfect spot for an ambush, but we would be coming up from behind, so ambush isn't our answer. But there's a steep grade getting to that pass and they would be goin' mighty slow with all that gold in the wagon."

Bull Morrison and Slim Calhoun walked into Ted Hickson's little offices at the Sierra Express Company building just about three o'clock. "I told Jory Anderson and Charley Green to stay at the hotel," Morrison said. "Right now, the town knows who we are but they don't know about those two." He had a nasty grin on his face.

"You're still lookin' to pick a fight, ain't you?' Calhoun had to chuckle remembering the swagger and hard talk at the saloon, the quick turn and gun in hand shaming the town marshal's deputy. "You're a piece, Bull Morrison. I'll ride with you anytime."

"You damn right I am, and damn right you will," he said, opening the door to Hickson's inner office, without knocking. "You here, Hickson?" he bellowed.

"Oh," Hickson said, looking up from his desk. "Oh, it's you, Marshal. Yes, come in, come in. Just two of you? I thought you were bringing more people. This is a precious cargo you'll be guarding."

"And we'll guard it well, Hickson. I understand you've ordered the wagon and teams?"

"Yes, a delivery wagon and three teams. There will be a teamster, and he'll have a boy with him, and I've scheduled everything to be ready to leave at four, tomorrow morning. You'll take the main road out of town and connect with the Walker River Road north to Carson City."

"This teamster and his helper are your employees?" Morrison didn't flinch when Hickson described which road to take. He and Calhoun already made plans to go the other way.

"Yes, yes. Been with us a long time. Name's Eddie Martin but most people call him Easy Eddie. Here's the paperwork you'll want for the officials at the U.S. Mint in Carson, and I'll sign off on these other papers in the morning when I turn the gold over to you." The sheaf of papers in Bull Morrison's hands were formal assay reports from each of the mines selling to the mint.

The mint would then run their own assays, and if the two agreed, the money would be transferred. If they didn't, an arbitration panel would determine how much money would be involved. That rarely happened as assaying was fairly accurate. "That'll be a heavy load, Hickson. We'll need good strong horses."

"Angus McMurray has some of the best stock in this part of the country, Marshal. I'm sure you'll have a fine trip." He walked from behind his desk to escort the two men out. "See you in the morning."

"I could handle a steak about this big and this thick," Morrison said as they walked down the main street of Aurora. "Occidental Hotel or Borealis Hotel? And fifteen potatoes, three loaves of bread, and a tureen of soup. What about you, Slim Calhoun?"

"Maybe about half of that," Calhoun laughed. "Let's get Jory and Charley and have a feast. Damn shame Angie doesn't serve supper. That venison stew I had for dinner was fine indeed. Like to get to know that skinny little twerp better. Bet she's a firecracker between the sheets."

"She screwed up my plans to whup on that toad of a deputy, Slim. I don't like her," he chuckled as they slipped into the Borealis Hotel to find the other deputies. "Nope, she ruined my afternoon, Calhoun. You'll need to find another woman." Calhoun was laughing all the way to the second floor to find Anderson and Green.

The four marshals took up a table for six in the Borealis dining room and ordered enough food for eight. Except for Calhoun, none had eaten since about five that morning. "You boys find out anything on your cruise around this berg?" Morrison asked. "Everything comes down at four in the morning."

Before either Anderson or Green could answer they were interrupted by a visitor. "Sorry to barge in like this, Marshal, but I think you need to know something."

"Tell me who you are and then tell me what I need to know," Morrison said. He did not offer a chair nor did he stand to greet the man. "You are aware that we are about to have our supper?"

"Up until yesterday's election I was Aurora City Marshal. Name's Ed Montgomery. There's a man in town we call Swampy. He cleans some of the saloons and sweeps the streets. Old man, but kinda the ears of the town. I learned over the years to pay attention to what he says."

"Yeah," Slim Calhoun said. "Montgomery. We were supposed to look you up but after meeting a lout named Olsen who's supposed to be a deputy city marshal we decided not to. He the reason you lost the election?"

"That's a thought," Montgomery said. "May I sit down, please?"

Morrison grumbled but motioned him to take a seat. "You talk, Montgomery and I'll eat." The steaks had come along with great bowls of mashed potatoes, and tureens of soup. "I'm listening."

"Jacob Swarthmore, Swampy, was sleeping in the warm grass alongside a warehouse that Silas Houston uses for storage when he heard men inside planning to rob a gold shipment scheduled to leave town tomorrow morning. Houston and that deputy you mentioned, Pete Olsen were two of the men."

"Now we're getting somewhere," Slim Calhoun said. "Damn right, Mr. Montgomery, that's what we want to hear. I'll bet you they were in the saloon, Bull, to do some plottin' and plannin' and you messed up their party." Bull Morrison just grumbled a bit between great bites of beef.

"According to Swampy, they are planning to follow you out of town and make their play along one of the roads. There's only two roads out of town."

"Did this Swampy feller mention how many

people would be making the attack?" Calhoun knew they had the four marshals and a company driver who would probably normally be an express guard.

"He couldn't see inside but said it sounded like maybe six or seven. This old man fed me information for many years, Marshal. I trust him."

"Well it's good for us to know these things," Calhoun said. "Why didn't you take this information to the city marshal?"

"I assume you're messin' with me since I just told you that Pete Olsen's involved. I may have lost the election, Marshal, but I've spent my life wearing a badge. I've worked Texas cow towns and Nevada mining camps, I've been on the Gulf and fought Mexicans, Marshal." He angered quickly and was about to stand to leave the table when Bull Morrison pulled himself away from a second steak.

"Sit quiet, Montgomery. You've done us a good turn and we appreciate it. We're a bit testy because of that fool Olsen, had a run in with him just a few hours ago. Do you know these roads around here well?"

"I do, indeed. Been here for several years now. The mountain over, over Lucky Boy Pass takes you down to Nine Mile Ranch and the larger, well-traveled road west takes you to the Walker River Road."

"If we were to take that well-traveled road, where would the best place to hit us be?" Morrison asked.

"Why, in the Walker River Canyon, or course. Road narrows way down, it's rocky as all get out. You gotta cross the river in several places. More than one shipment has been hijacked there."

"And that other road? Over Lucky Boy Pass?" Asking about both roads didn't give anything away and Morrison was getting a good education on the area.

"There's a long and steep hill, lots of turns, lots of rocks, leading up to the pass. Slow you down right away. Good spot for an attack," Montgomery said. "There's mining in that area but not very many people."

"Would you do us one more favor, Mr. Montgomery? You and Swampy keep all this information close to your vest. We've heard some good rumors about a hit, and yours rings far more likely than anything else we've heard. Don't give it away that we know about a hit."

"I would never do that, Marshal. One more thing, they said they were going to wait until you pulled out of town, so they would know which road you would be on, then follow and hit you from behind."

"Typical coward outlaws," Calhoun murmured.

Montgomery stood to leave and Morrison stood with him, shook his hand and the group watched the former city marshal walk out the door. "Sounds like it's time for us to make a little plan," Bull Morrison said.

"Too many ears around here," Calhoun said. "Let's wander toward the stables, maybe have a chat with McMurray. He seems to know a lot about what goes on in this town."

CHAPTER FIVE

Wendell Harrison locked up the mine company offices and stepped out onto the long boardwalk enjoying thoughts about the coming morning. He'd been a patient man for several years, waiting for the mine owners to recognize his abilities and offer him a better position or an ownership opportunity. He'd been passed over for the last time, he thought. This time it was a slap in the face, a full embarrassment and repudiation of his worth to the company.

He was the mill foreman, a good position, was paid well, and given company housing to boot. He wanted that superintendent's desk in the worst way. It had prestige written all over it and one thing that impressed Wendell Harrison was a man who walked around with prestige written all over him. The company made a formal and very public announcement that they were bringing in a man from Virginia City who had more mining and milling experience than any ten men in Aurora.

"They'll never shame me in public again," he murmured. "I'm the foreman but should have been named superintendent. Well, they'll understand just how I feel when they hear their precious shipment has gone missing." He had a grand smile on his face when he entered the Occidental Saloon and made his way toward the gaming tables in the rear. In his mind he was already a mining nabob, a mover and shaker, but after tomorrow, he would close his little clapboard house, pack what few things he would need, and head for Mexico, to live like the king he knew he was.

"A nice little fishing village, my bed always warm with lovely dusky ladies, plenty of tequila and whiskey is my future," he found himself muttering. Of course it would be far better if he didn't have to split all that gold and silver with so many others. Maybe, he thought, it was time to devise a way to get most of the gold for himself. He had never shot a man, for that matter had only been in one fight in his life, and didn't do well at that. No, he thought, he had gotten where he was by way of good thinking and it would be good thinking that would get him most of the gold.

"The louts Houston hired can be dealt with easy enough. Smaller cuts and they wouldn't know the difference, but cutting out Pete Olsen will be the deal. I'll get Olsen in a fight with Houston or one of the hired guns and hope for the best. Maybe join the fray." he smiled at the thought.

Harrison looked toward the dining area before settling on which table game he would play and saw Angie Whitaker sitting alone at one of the tables. "She's rough around the edges, opinionated to a fault, but would make a fine traveling companion," he murmured. He made what he considered a most casual approach to Angie's table.

"Oh, my, Miss Whitaker," he said in mock surprise. "It's so nice to see you. Eating alone, are you?"

"Hello, Wendell," she said. "Yes, I am. I tend to fancy my own company, and particularly when I don't have to do the cooking." Angela had had more than one unpleasant evening with Wendell Harrison, to the point of demanding he leave on one occasion and wasn't about to have another. She was, instead thinking of a tall, broad shouldered U.S. Marshal.

That was a bit rude, Harrison thought and put aside the possibility of asking Angela Whitaker to take a long adventure to Mexico with him. "I say," he said, bowed stiffly, and returned to the faro table. "Most annoying," he muttered. "There are finer, more enjoyable companions to find, I'm sure."

Angela Whitaker had a smile on her face as she watched the arrogant mining man straighten up and almost march into the saloon. "He's almost as rude and proud of himself as Pete Olsen. It would be nice if those marshals came in for supper about now."

Harrison wasn't a gambler and lost the first couple of hands, stood up and walked out of the saloon. "I think I will spend the rest of the evening planning how to get most of that gold for myself after our attack tomorrow. Those five men Olsen and Houston hired must be gotten rid of." He had it in the back of his mind that maybe even Houston could be taken out of the picture somehow.

"The thing is, Bull, there are four of us plus the driver and seven or eight of them. For us, that puts the odds in our favor. We've always been outgunned and we win because we usually outthink the bad guys." Slim Calhoun had a smile on his face as the four marshals sat around the potbelly stove in Angus McMurray's barn office. McMurray had been invited to sit in on their planning talk since he knew the country so well.

"We know which road we're taking and they don't," he continued. "Angus has told us the same thing that Montgomery said. That they would probably hit us somewhere on that long steep climb to Lucky Boy Pass. With four up and a heavily laden wagon, we would be sitting ducks out there."

"Yeah," Bull Morrison growled. "But if two of us dropped off and waited for this so-called gang to ride on past us, and if the wagon pulled off into some rocks before they got to that long steep climb, and those left with the wagon set up a strong line of defense, you know, ambush," and he smiled that horrible smile of his. "We could wipe their rotten butts from the face of the earth."

"Catch 'em in a cross fire," Angus McMurray chuckled. "Well, hell, that ain't fair." Morrison howled with delight, whopping McMurray hard enough to knock the big blacksmith back a step or two.

"Charley," Bull said to Green, "you hold back and ride with Slim. Jory, you stay with me and the wagon. Now, Mr. Blacksmith, sir, you tell me where best to pull this ambush off. You say you know that road like the path to your bed."

"I do. Indeed I do," McMurray chuckled. He sat down at the desk and drew a map of the trail leading out of Aurora toward Lucky Boy Pass and pinpointed a spot where there would be a blind turn around a rock formation. "It looks like a European castle as you ride toward it and just past the turn there's a stand of pine and aspen." He put an X to mark the spot. "All the room in the world to hide that wagon and teams and an open field of fire for the ambush."

"I like that. Field of fired indeed. You got some military in your background, Mr. McMurray. Yes sir, that's good. They come around that castle wall and we light into them, they turn to find cover and Slim, you nail their butts good. It would be nice to have a prisoner or two but if it's them or you, make it them that goes to the deep down under." Morrison stood closer to the stove, smiling, looking right at Angus McMurray. "Old Slim there," he drawled out, trying to sound like Slim, "told me you had some of Kentucky's finest tucked away near here."

McMurray smiled back, opened a drawer and pulled a bottle of bourbon out. "Cups are hanging on the wall there, Bull."

Bull had just gotten everyone's cups filled when gunshots and screaming came from the Borealis Hotel Saloon, just down the street from the barns. Bull and Slim were out the door at a run, the other deputies working to keep up. "That's a woman screaming," Morrison said watching Slim Calhoun's long legs outdistance him quickly. "Right behind you, Pard."

Several men had bolted out of the saloon and Calhoun had to shoulder his way past them and through the swinging doors. Pete Olsen was standing at the end of the bar, weapon in hand and two men were on the floor, one not moving, the other in great pain. Calhoun pulled up short and stood quiet as Morrison and the other deputies came up behind him.

"What's this all about, Olsen?" Calhoun took one step forward.

"Ain't none of your concern, Marshal. This is town business." He waved his pistol to some of those standing by to get the body out of the saloon, and to get the wounded man on his feet. Olsen did not put his weapon back in its holster. Two women who spent time with men gambling and drinking were crying, sobbing actually, at one of the cocktail tables.

"What happened?" Calhoun asked again.

"Back off, Marshal. Ain't none of your damn business." Anger was a poison that spread through the deputy, anger at being questioned about anything he did, anger at knowing that at least one of the men glaring at him had already outdrawn him in public. He snarled at the locals staring at the wounded and dead. "Get these men out of here." He turned to Calhoun. "Don't rile me, Marshal. This is town marshal business and I'm the man here."

"Anybody think to call the town marshal over?" Slim looked around at the crowd. He had the slightest grin on his face and took a short step to the bar just as Angie Whitaker came dashing through from the restaurant. "My God," she said. "Pete, what have you done? That's Ed Riley bleeding all over the floor. Ed, what happened? Oh, no, Ed, what did he do?" She bent down next to the wounded man, moving a couple of the men aside who were going to take him to jail. Ed Riley was an elderly man, probably well over sixty and well liked in town.

"Olsen shot me and Roddy cuz we wouldn't make room for him at the bar. Got all angry and dumb like he does," Riley moaned. He was grimacing as pain from the bullet wound that slashed through his chest. Angie could see blood pumping from a hole in the middle of the man's shirt and started to rip Riley's shirt to help stem the flow.

Olsen reached down and grabbed the girl by the shoulder and jerked her away from the wounded man. "He's my prisoner, Angie. Stay away from him."

"Ed Riley is sixty years old, Pete," she stammered. "He's all stove up from working in the mines. You shot him? Why? He wouldn't hurt nobody, never," she cried. She was furious and the crying made her even more angry. She was trying to get free of the deputy and he was holding her tight.

"Let go. That hurts. You're nothing but a killer and outlaw yourself, Pete Olsen." Angie was crying and Slim Calhoun stepped quickly to her side.

"Let her go, Olsen," he said, ever so quietly. His eyes locked onto his, were narrowed little slits offering a quick death, and Olsen felt a strong hand take hold of his arm. Olsen let Angie go, stepped back fast and raised his weapon, cocked and ready to kill.

Those standing close could hear the bone break when a rifle barrel slammed onto the arm holding the big Colt. The yowling of pain was heard throughout the saloon. "Don't you ever pull a weapon on a U.S. Marshal, mister," Charley Green said, nudging Olsen away from Angie and Calhoun with his rifle barrel. "You even twitch and you're a dead man."

Olsen was bent over holding his broken arm, Calhoun picked up the dropped Colt, and Angie bent down again to help Ed Riley. "Who's the dead man?" Calhoun asked.

Ed Riley was still gasping for air and wheezed out the name Roddy Simpson. Simpson, like Riley was an old miner and prospector, had a claim up toward the Lucky Boy Pass that kept him in whiskey and beans and had never been in any kind of trouble, according to Angie Whitaker. "The town's deputy city marshal shoots two old men because they wouldn't make room for him at the bar?

"Damn me, Bull Morrison, but I don't think that's a federal offense. We don't seem to have any jurisdiction here," he chuckled. "Maybe just shoot the bastard and go on about our business."

Angie was crying but was able to get the flow of blood stemmed, Bull Morrison and Charley Green had Pete Olsen well covered, and Slim Calhoun took a good look at Roddy Simpson's body.

"This man was shot in the back," he said. Calhoun stood up and stepped to the bar to face the town deputy. "Olsen, you are one serious piece of crap. An old man crippled from years in the mines shot down like a dog and his friend shot in the back. Let's go, boy," he said, cuffing him and forcing him toward the doors.

Olsen screamed in pain when his broken arm was twisted up behind him and the cuffs were snapped in place. "That don't hurt half as much as it should, boy. Any man who wears a badge and shoots an unarmed man in the back should feel as much pain as is possible.

I'm gonna see to it that you fully understand what pain is, boy."

"Where you taking him?" Angie asked. "You gonna hang that dog? Or just walk him out and shoot the bastard?" She reddened quickly realizing what she'd said and ducked her head down to work on Ed Riley.

"Taking him to jail," Slim said.

"Won't do no good," she said. "Conrad Wilson will just set him free as soon as you walk out."

"Maybe so but I'll have the pleasure of getting' him there." He gave her a big smile and continued. "Course, you did have a couple of good ideas." Pete Olsen was standing with his head hanging down, flinching at the pain spreading from his broken arm. Can one suffering from paranoia and known as a psychotic killer suffer from shock as well?

"That boy's gonna pass out on you, Slim." Bull Morrison chuckled, poking Olsen near the broken bone. "Better get him a cell where he'll be warm and safe from us bullies. Run along now," he laughed. Calhoun was chuckling, pushing Olsen along and out the door.

"WELL? Did you get that nasty deputy all jailed up?" Morrison, Green, Anderson, and Angie were sitting at a table near the front of the saloon when Slim Calhoun returned from the town marshal's office.

"He's probably already out, Bull. That town

marshal is truly a fool. Nothing we can do about that, but it does change what might happen in the morning."

"It could," Morrison said. "I don't think it will change our plans though. The doc came and took Ed Riley off saying he'd live, but Roddy Simpson died immediately. Can't picture a man wearing a badge shooting a man in the back. Maybe you should have just shot the deputy, Mr. Green."

"Yup," is all Charley Green said. "Me and Jory are gonna sleep at the stables, Bull. That way we'll be there when the mines bring the gold and silver in." He stopped short realizing that Angie Whitaker was at the table.

"Oh, fiddle," she laughed. "Whole damn town knows about the shipment going out tomorrow. That crazy Childers and Balderdash Emory have been talking about it for a week now. I should have known that's why you boys are here. I thought it was cuz of my good cookin'." She looked Calhoun straight in the eyes with a grand smile.

"That had a lot to do with it," Slim chuckled. "On that note, the doc had Olsen's arm in a cast but I noticed that he had a little Remington tucked in his waist band that could be pulled with his left hand. He might not be out of tomorrow's party."

"Angie," Bull Morrison said. "You mentioned a couple of names, Balderdash something, and Childers. Tell me what you know about them." He looked at Slim Calhoun, then Charley Green. "I remember Ed

Montgomery telling us his story. The name Balderdash was definitely used."

"Balderdash Emory wants to be an outlaw but don't know how," Angie laughed. "He robbed the stage and came right back to town and got drunk telling the world all about it. Dumb, dumb, dumb," she laughed some more. "Childers ain't much smarter. You men are thinking that Pete Olsen is planning on holding up your shipment, eh? Well, Pete's just dumb enough to hire Balderdash and Childers."

"If there were others that Olsen might hire for a gang, who might they be?" Charley Green was trying to be careful asking the question.

Angie laughed right out at the way he said it. "Now, Mr. Green, you just look around this old saloon and most of the others in our old camp here, and there are men with papers out on them in every one. You could find bank robbers, stagecoach robbers, burglars, and a murderer or two by the end of a short walk about town."

"Sure glad there's four of us," Slim Calhoun chuckled.

———————————

CHAPTER SIX

"You've got us in a hell of a mess now," Silas Houston was stomping around the old barn, cussing up a tornado of a storm at Pete Olsen. The idea of the man being the lead gun of the group went out the window when he walked in wearing a cast on his gun arm, wearing bruises on his once angry face, and his slouched posture. "Our one big chance at being rich for the rest of our lives and you do something more stupid than even old Harrison could think of. We might have to forget this job, you fool."

"You watch your mouth, Silas," Olsen said. It wasn't the same Pete Olsen saying it, Houston noted. No swagger. No real threat in those words. His right arm in a sling and a useless Colt on his right hip didn't intimidate Silas Houston one bit.

"Ain't nothin' changed. I can ride and shoot better than anyone else, so back off. Get with the others and have them spread around town and ready to mount up when that wagon leaves the barns. We'll leave out quietly and not together and meet up about two miles out of town, whichever road they take."

Silas Houston was still furious with the young deputy, sure that his foolish actions would keep him from being rich the rest of his life. "You say you can shoot better than anyone else? Draw, damn you," Houston yelled and pulled his sidearm, watching Olsen's eyes widen in fear, unable to pull his gun. "Now, Pete Olsen, do you understand the damage you've done to our plans?

"Does Harrison know what you've done?"

"Ain't none of his concern," Olsen snapped. "Now get out here and get with the others. I'm gonna sleep here tonight."

"No you ain't," Houston said. "Go home and get some sleep." Houston cussed under his breath the whole walk to the Occidental on Pine Street and found Jake Jackson and Childers at the bar. "Let's take a table," Houston said. "We need to talk without other ears pickin' up on us." He grabbed a bottle, laid down a coin and they walked to a table near the front of the long narrow saloon.

It was still early in the evening and the louder, wilder, sometimes more dangerous crowd hadn't yet arrived. Gambling tables were only about half-filled, the ladies of the night were not getting much attention, and old Oily James (The Senator) Smithson was pounding away on his piano to no one's amusement.

"Pete Olsen killed old Roddy Simpson and shot Ed Riley tonight. Federal marshals busted him up pretty good," Houston said after they got seated. "Dumb bastard has a broken arm."

"Well, now," Jake Jackson said. He sat back in his chair, chomped some on a cold cigar, took a long drink of whiskey, and continued in his slow drawl. "That ain't so good. We ain't gonna hit the shipment? Ain't gonna be filthy rich?"

"Take it easy, Jake. The hit is still on but Olsen might not be in his best condition. The marshals broke his gun arm. It's important that we all know that. We might not be able to depend on him like we would want to." Houston's face would have told anyone around that he didn't believe a word he was saying. Olsen might not be in any condition to hold up a wagonload of gold defended by a bunch of U.S. Marshals. Might not be the least bit dependable.

Houston had to keep the group together, keep their spirits up and ready to make the biggest hit any of them had ever thought of. How could he do that when Olsen wasn't going to be the big gun? Olsen and he put this whole thing together when Harrison told them about the shipment.

"It will be up to us to pull this off," Silas said. "Remember, have your horses saddled and ready before that wagon moves off. Drift out of town alone.

We'll meet up about two miles out of town and then take out the marshals and get the gold.

"We'll take them at the Walker River Canyon if they go the river road north. We have to stay strong on this. I can't imagine just how much money each of us is going to have at this same time tomorrow night." Silas Houston was afraid of losing what he didn't have and knew he had to keep these men thinking positive.

"You two get with Payson and West. And Emory, you make sure everyone knows what we're supposed to do." Silas Houston should have been filled with the excitement of what tomorrow would bring. Gold. Hundreds of pounds of gold so close he could almost touch it. Enough for him to move east and live well, dress as a gentleman, and drink as one. Instead, he felt a heavy load of doom fall on his shoulders knowing that Pete Olsen had let them down.

"I won't let that fool boy's temper take this from me." Harrison exploded when Houston told him about what Pete Olsen had done. They were sitting in Harrison's shanty on the edge of the mining property, drinking whiskey. The shanty was provided by the company and Harrison hated it even more than he hated the men who had denied him his position in the company.

"Silas, this is our only chance to be rich for the rest of our lives. That gold is in twelve-ounce ingots, in crates, Silas, and ready for us to take it. One pound Troy bars, Silas. Four hundred dollars is what each little bar of gold is worth and that damn hothead has closed the door on our opportunity."

"No!" Houston stood quickly and walked to the stove. "No, Wendell, the door is not closed. We still have those men with their guns and they're still ready. We will take that shipment of gold and we will do it with or without Pete Olsen."

"There would be one less mouth to feed, so to speak," Harrison smiled. "Do you think the others will still go through with this hit if Olsen is out? Are they his men or ours? Have you talked with any of them?" Harrison kept getting flashes of crates of gold bars flying off into nothingness, away, away, in a dream cloud. "I won't give this opportunity up because of Olsen's stupidity."

"The only one who might foul up the works would be Balderdash Emory. That man has to be certified as an idiot, but he is the best gunman of the bunch. Fearless, probably because he's too stupid to understand fear, and incredibly fast and accurate with a pistol and a rifle.

"I've talked with Childers and Jackson, and everything's still set for tomorrow morning." He sat back and poured another healthy shot of liquor. "Is the gold still on schedule?"

"Yes," Harrison said. "The mines will have it at the stables before four and the wagon is scheduled out at four. Brady Throckmorton said that Ted Hickson himself will be at the stables to see to it the gold is loaded and accounted for."

"Wish I could be there to see that," Houston said. He smiled, poured another shot of whiskey, and said, "But it will be more fun when we unload that wagon. You still planning to take it to that ranch down in the valley?"

"The ranch you're thinking of is in that long valley along the Walker River, but we don't really know which road the wagon is going to be on. No, Silas, the best bet is to get the wagon hidden somewhere, unload it and distribute the ingots, and burn the wagon. Everyone's on their own after that."

"There's no doubt in your mind that we have to kill the marshals and the driver?"

"No, Silas, no doubt. We can't let anyone live. We're too well known and anyone could identify us. No, Silas. No witnesses."

He had a smile on his face thinking of a long, quiet ride down that long Owens Valley, across the desert and into Mexico. "I have two mules ready to pack, Mr. Houston. How about you?"

"I'll stay here until I sell my business, then it's New York City for me. Maybe travel through Europe for a few years. Yes, Mr. Harrison, it will be a grand pleasure to unload that wagon."

Balderdash Emory was incensed when Childers told him about what Pete Olsen had done. "So maybe we should just shoot that badge toting boy and take his share." He, Childers, Jackson, Payson, and West were in the Borealis Saloon sharing a bottle going over the next morning's plans.

"Silas Houston said everything's still on, it's just that we can't depend on Olsen's guns."

"Balderdash. We've never been able to count on that boy. So, what do we do?" Emory sat back with a smug look on his face and answered his own question. "I think we should hit that gold shipment when it arrives at the stables. Why chase it all over these mountains?"

The four men at the table stopped drinking and muttering. Balderdash Emory may have hit on a good plan. It was Tiny West who put a damper on the idea. "There are U.S. Marshals guarding that gold."

"Oh, yeah, sure there are," Emory said. "I think the same ones that would be on the wagon if we hit it out there on the road somewhere. If we can take them out there on the road somewhere we can sure as hell take them at McMurray's stables."

"What about Silas and Mr. Harrison? They will be somewhere in town on their horses waiting for the wagon to leave. Shouldn't they be in on this idea of yours, Emory?"

"Balderdash! When that gold arrives from the various mines to be loaded on the big wagon is when we should hit it. We can ride in as a group. Just look at us. We're all good with our guns. We ride in, kill those marshals before they even know we're there, grab as much of the gold as we can and ride like lightning in four different directions."

"Old Emory's got himself worked up pretty good on this," Eddie Payson said. He lit a cheroot and sat back thinking about the plan. "Houston and Harrison are waiting somewhere for the wagon to leave, God only knows where Olsen will be, and we swoop in like hawks on a rabbit and take the gold."

"I think we need to get out of this saloon and go somewhere that we won't be heard, and get this all worked out," Tiny West said. "Too damn many ears around here."

"Let's get some sleep and meet behind Houston's warehouse about three. That way, whatever we decide will be fresh when we hit." Childers said.

"Balderdash. Let's get it worked out now," Emory exploded.

"There's still the problem of those marshals," Jake Jackson said. "What I heard was that one of them outdrew Pete Olsen and it was another that broke his arm. On the road is one thing. That's an ambush, and I like that. But, riding in straight up against U.S. Marshals? Whew."

"There's five of us, Jake," Eddie Payson said. "We're all damn good with our guns, and we'll surprise them the same as an ambush. I think old Balderdash has himself a good plan. We won't have to split nothing with nobody."

"If we hold up the wagon on the road we get the whole wagon full," Jackson said. "If we hit the stables we only get what we can carry on our horses."

"Which is probably more than Harrison would give us in the first place," Balderdash laughed.

"Yup," Tiny West said. "I'd bet Harrison and Houston are already planning how to cut our share. You know damn well that Olsen would in a quick turn of an ace. I vote with Balderdash."

Within less than a minute they all agreed, stood and nodded to each other and headed out for needed sleep. "See you behind the warehouse," was Balderdash's last words to the group.

"We need to have a little talk, Bull. I've got one of those feelings again." Slim Calhoun and Bull Morrison were walking down the dimly lit hallway toward their hotel rooms. "You know how those are."

"Yeah, I do," Bull said. "The last time you had one of those feelings I got shot in the leg. All right, then, let's hear it. I've got a bottle in my room."

Bull was sitting on the edge of the bed and Slim was at a writing desk, each with a tin cup full of whiskey. "What if what we heard from Ed Montgomery has been changed? What if they hit us at the stables? Me and Charley Green would be out on the road somewhere leaving you and Jory alone at the stables."

"Damn, damn, damn," Morrison said, over and over. "You and your damn feelings. Sumbitch. You could be really right, too. That's why you're my deputy. To keep me alive."

Bull Morrison was aware that what he said might not be an untruth. He and Calhoun had ridden together for so many years, been in so many big gun fights with ugly and dangerous outlaws, and he knew that often they came out on top because of Calhoun's strange way of thinking through a situation.

"If they did change their plans, the one's we think we know about, that would put their eight guns against me and Jory Anderson. Jory's good but he ain't as good as you, old man." Bull Morrison reached for the bottle and filled their cups. "Eight guns against two. Still good odds for us old marshals, but I'd rather have you and Charley alongside me and Jory."

"In the event they didn't hit the stables, me and Charley could still ride out with the wagon and then drop off somewhere in order to follow whoever might follow. I don't like the thought of you against eight. Me and you, that's different," Calhoun laughed.

"Yeah, like at Spanish Wells," Morrison chuckled. "You, me, and that Mexican kid with the slingshot against half of all the Mexican outlaws in the country." He pulled up his arm, hand open and finger splayed. "I lost a finger that day."

"Yes you did, Marshal Bull Morrison. And you brought four Mexican banditos to our favorite little jail in San Ysidro where they were hanged. You might remember saving my life in the process," Calhoun laughed.

"Yeah, a man does have a few regrets in life. Go to bed, Calhoun, and we'll set up for an ambush in the morning. It's late and I'm tired. Besides that, my missing finger hurts."

CHAPTER SEVEN

Silas Houston was a good businessman, ran his business in such a manner as giving himself a good return on investment while appearing to give his customers fair prices for well made goods. Part of the reason for a fat profit margin was that he didn't always purchase the goods he was selling. Some were appropriated, by way of a shotgun or cocked revolver, along the roads leading to Aurora. At least that's what many believed.

Wendell Harrison on the other hand was a miner with no business background. He knew rocks well, could read ore bearing structure in the ways of a geologist. He was ego driven, arrogant, and rather haughty toward what he considered the lower classes.

What the two men had in common was a great desire to be wealthy beyond compare coupled with a lack of personal morals. To steal, acquire, have was far more important than just how it was accomplished. Neither man had close friends nor wanted them. Houston was married, but in name only while Harrison had never taken the chance.

Often, men were driven to criminal acts by whiskey, or women, or both, but these men were driven by the simple words, greed and ego. Both believed they had the right to be filthy rich and damn those who stood in the way.

While neither man held strong personal ethics, neither was a full time criminal either. Thus the idea of those they hired turning on them wasn't in the cards. "Will those five men you hired be able to pull this off with little help from Olsen?" Harrison wasn't sure that Olsen would even show up. "This isn't going the way we planned it, Houston."

"Olsen has really messed this up but I think those men know that you and I are who put this together, that Olsen was just another gun." Houston walked to a window and noticed the sky lightening just a bit. "Mid-summer sunrise coming up, Wendell. Time for all good men to go to work."

Harrison had to chuckle over that. "Our work awaits, Silas. Indeed it does. Should we stick together or not?"

"We've got the men scattered all over town and asked them to ride out singly, and I think we should do the same. I'll go up to my feed store and saddle up. You can saddle up and ride right from your house here. You can see the stables and so will I. Just wait a few minutes after the wagon pulls out to follow. See you down the trail, Wendell."

The two men shook hands, as business men should, and Harrison watched Houston walk out and down the street toward his feed store. He took a long drink of whiskey and felt it boil its way down. Fear filled the mining man. Would he really be able to shoot another human being? Stealing the gold would be the easy part, killing another man might be impossible.

The marshals and those tending the wagon had to die. There could not be witnesses left to talk about the robbery. At the same time, if Harrison was to get as much of that gold as he wanted, some or most of his accomplices must die as well. The thought of simply pointing a gun at a man and shooting him dead frightened Harrison far more than the thought of being caught and sent to prison.

He walked out the door and around to the carriage house in the back of the old cabin, saddled his horse, and sat on his haunches in the doorway, looking down the long street to McMurray's stables at the end of the street. He pulled his pocket watch, gave it a quick wind or two and saw that it was just three thirty.

"Gold should be getting loaded at the mines about now. Our load will be the largest but each mine has done well this month. The mint is doing me a favor asking for the one-pound troy bars instead of the larger ingots we usually sell each month. My first purchase with that wonderful gold will be a high prancing team of coach horses and a landau for them to pull."

He chuckled, opened his coat and pulled the heavy revolver to check one more time that it was loaded and ready to fire. He walked around the horse and pulled his rifle and checked it as well. "I would feel so much better if that fool Olsen hadn't been so stupid. The night before the biggest heist in Aurora's history and he shoots two men and gets whupped on by U.S. Marshals. Damn that boy. Will he even show up?" The muttering continued as the mining man watched the sky slowly lighten.

PETE OLSEN TOSSED and turned on the little cot at Houston's warehouse and after a half hour of that gave up, dressed, and headed for his own little cabin tucked behind the city marshal's jail. "The first thing I'm gonna do is kill that deputy marshal. I don't give a damn about the gold, not like Houston and Harrison, but I do give a damn about that marshal dying. Hard. He has to die hard, gut shot, bleeding out slow," and he laughed softly settling into his bed.

If asked a week before this he would have told you that nothing was more important than having that gold. Being publicly shamed, first by Bull Morrison, then by

Slim Calhoun, changed the picture. His mind was warped by anyone's standards and because of that he was far more than just a dangerous criminal. He no longer was able to think, everything he did was reaction, not thought.

He was almost asleep when there was a soft rap on the door. He pulled his Colt from the gunbelt hanging on a chair next to the bed and crept to the door. "What?" he said from the side of the door.

"It's Brady. It's important, Pete, let me in."

"It better be," Olsen said letting Throckmorton in. "I was sleepin'." He pulled his pants on and slipped into his boots. "What's so important this time of night?"

"Ted Hickson hired Easy Eddie Martin to drive the wagon. He's wicked with that shotgun of his and always carries a rifle too."

"Yeah, Easy Eddie, eh? Well, one more gun ain't gonna matter none, Brady. Anybody else know this? Don't want to spook those boys. I ain't afraid of Easy Eddie or anyone else," Olsen snarled. "All I want is that marshal at the end of my gun barrel."

"I haven't talked to anyone. Well, Angie's firing up her stoves right now and I had coffee with her, but didn't tell her nothin'. Just a woman."

"She might die, too. Prettying up with that marshal. You sure you didn't say nothin'. I'll kill you where you stand if you give us up, Brady."

"No, Pete, no. I promise, I didn't say nothin' to

nobody. Hickson ordered the three teams and large wagon, like I told you, then hired Easy Eddie to drive the teams. I guess McMurray will provide the handler. Everything's just like I told you and I ain't told nobody nothin'." Brady Throckmorton was a wisp of a man, worked behind a desk at the express office every day of the week, didn't drink, hadn't been with a woman in three years, and was terrified of Pete Olsen.

"I told you that I would give you some of that gold if you did what I asked, Brady, and I will. But if I find out you been talkin', I'll kill you dead. Now, get out of here." Throckmorton didn't wait to be told twice. Olsen walked to the door to make sure the man was gone.

"Looks like the sun be coming up and that means it's time to get ready. Sure would like to just ride into that stables and shoot that marshal." He was still chuckling about that as he strapped his gunbelt on and checked the Colt for its load. It took three tries to get the belt hitched because of his broken arm and the cast that held it. The chuckles turned to curses filled with hatred of Slim Calhoun and little Angela Whitaker. "She was all flirtin' with that marshal and he was all getting' up and tough for her, and I get a broken arm. I'm gonna kill 'em both this morning."

Olsen couldn't see the stables from his cabin, so after saddling his horse he rode around to the front of the building and tied off. He walked into the jail and stirred the fire up to make a pot of coffee. That done, he grabbed the old chair from behind the desk and propped it up on the boardwalk outside to sit and watch for the sunrise. "Hell, just like old Ed Montgomery," he chuckled.

"Should see those wagons from the mines come through soon," he mumbled, leaning back some. He could see Angie's café down the street and felt the hate rise again, saw Houston's feed and supply store, and watched a drunk try three times to get into the Borealis Saloon before realizing the doors were locked. "Ed Montgomery said this was the best time of the day. Ed Montgomery's an idiot. The best time of the day is when you can hurt somebody real good. Somebody that tried to hurt you."

He was checking his watch for the third time when he spotted the first of the mine company wagons pulling down the street for the livery. "Right on time, boys," he muttered. He waved to driver as he went by. "Glad you're bringin' my gold in boys," he said quietly.

"A LITTLE EARLY THIS MORNING, eh girl?" Jacob Swarthmore bowed slightly to the lady as she came down the boardwalk. Swarthmore had swamped two saloons and was on his job of cleaning the town's boardwalks. "It's gonna be hot today."

"Good morning to you, Jacob. Yup, a little early. I'll

have coffee hot in a short time. Y'awl come on back for a cup, will you?"

"Obliged, Ma'am," Swarthmore said. He came west as a young man straight out Harvard and practiced frontier law from Missouri to Texas, from Ohio to Oregon, and learned the hard way that the best law is not practiced from the open end of a whiskey bottle. Swarthmore was nearing seventy, broke as broke as a man could get, but still acted the gentleman to all women, said sir and ma'am, and wore clean clothes. He may have been a broken man but he still had his pride.

"Seems more people moving around this morning than usual," she said.

"Must be the late summer mornings, Miss. Old Mr. Sol gets up mighty early this time of the year, and our fair city, named after the goddess of dawn, greets him gaily."

"You're a bit of a poet and philosopher this morning, Jacob," she laughed. She opened the door to her café and got started on her early morning chores. After getting the fires lit in the stoves and coffee started, she glanced out the window and watched Jacob walk down the street in front of the city marshal's office, which brought back memories of Pete Olsen's shooting the night before.

"That was a horrible thing he did last night," she muttered. "Old Roddy Simpson dead and Ed Riley shot up an' hurtin'. Damn little boy," she said a bit louder than a mutter.

"What was that?"

She spun around almost spilling her cup of fresh coffee. "Oh, Mr. Throckmorton, you scared me half to death."

"I'm so sorry, Angie. I thought you heard me come in and was speaking to me. I certainly didn't mean to frighten you. Seems quite a few people up early today. Is the coffee ready?"

"Yes, of course. Here, sit down and I'll get you a cup. Fire's ain't hot enough to cook on yet, though, if you're thinkin' of breakfast."

"Looks like it's gonna be a hot one. I thought I'd come down and watch the mine company wagons deliver the gold to the stables."

"That's right," Angie said. "That shipment goes out this morning. Maybe those marshals will come in for coffee before they ride off. Did you get to meet them?"

"Saw two of them at the office but didn't say nothin'. That's Hickson's job. He don't like me talkin' to people. Says talk ain't good for the express business. Well, thanks for the coffee, I better be moving along."

She walked him to the door and closed it after him. "I'll keep an eye on the stables and when I see Slim and them arrive I'll bring 'em some good hot coffee. I'll fill a sack with sourdough biscuits for 'em take on their ride. I'd sure like to ride with that Slim Calhoun for a couple of months or years." Her morning chores were filled with happy thoughts and many smiles that morning.

Mornings were busy as miners, shopkeepers, and a

stray outlaw or two started arriving between four thirty and five, and the lady had a wonderful reputation in the area for putting out good victuals along with a pleasant atmosphere. "Old Brady was right, there's people all over town and it ain't even four o'clock. Still cold in the morning but it's gonna be a hot one today."

CHAPTER EIGHT

"It's getting' light, boys. Time to get up," Tiny West said, kicking bedrolls as he walked down the aisle at Houston's old barn warehouse. "There's a pot of gold waitin' for us." Several bottles of bad whiskey along with ideas of how to spend all the gold they planned to steal meant a short night for sleep. Tiny had to kick Balderdash twice to get him to even grumble out a slurred "Balderdash."

There were few high clouds starting to show a touch of pink far to the east and just a hint of chill to the morning air. Summer was being eased out and fall in the mountains of western Nevada could often be spelled winter. None of those boys would have noticed.

"It's getting light fast and those wagons from the mines will be arriving in the next fifteen minutes or so.

If you're not on your horse in five minutes you won't be invited to the party," West grumbled. "Let's go."

Jake Jackson was first in the saddle followed by West, Payson, and Childers. Balderdash Emory was slow but rode out with the group as they headed down Pine Street to the stables. "Let's keep as close to the dark side of the street as possible. Sure as hell don't want to get there before the gold does." Tiny West had taken command of the group and no one had challenged him. It may have been Balderdash's plan but it was West giving the orders.

Every man knew that Pete Olsen should be driving this herd but also knew that it was a typical failing by Olsen for him not being the leader. Jackson, Payson, and Childers were followers and had always been followers. There wasn't a lick of creativity in any of them, while Balderdash was simply a hanger-on, willing to do whatever anyone else wanted to do. His little flares of creativity were accidents of nature.

"Childers, why don't you casually ride on out there and around the block and see what's going on. I can't tell from here," West said. "Olsen or Houston should have figured this out yesterday," he said and then caught himself. Yesterday, he remembered, they weren't planning to hit the shipment at the stables. Childers stepped down from his gelding and handed the reins to Jackson.

"Think I'll see more if I walk out there," he said. He made the short walk to the corner and stood quietly in the shadows watching the McMurray stables and livery. Whatever was going on, it was either inside the barns or in the corrals and stockyards out behind them. He walked back to his horse.

"Can't see nothin' goin' on," he said.

"We'll just wait here for the wagons to go by and then hit them. Now's a good time to check your weapons for full loads and tighten your cinches." West liked this idea of being the boss. He thought it would be good to have a real gang of good gunmen and hit some of the banks around these mining camps. There was a lot of money in Bodie, in Carson City, and of course in Virginia City.

During the night he had brought the idea up to Eddie Payson and Childers but they weren't much interested. Payson said something about taking his share of this gold and heading to San Francisco while Childers just said a quick no. "Men with no vision, no thought of the future," West murmured. "I need men to ride with me who can see themselves rolling in gold."

BULL MORRISON and Slim Calhoun walked into McMurray's barns wiping sleep from their eyes. Jory Anderson and Charley Green spent the night at the stables and met them with a pot of hot coffee. "Now we're talking," Morrison said. "Where's McMurray?"

"Helping to harness the teams," Charley Green

said. "The teamster is here, too. He looks more like a desperado than a teamster. Says his name is Easy Eddie Martin. I don't remember seeing any broadsheets with that name, but you might want to talk to him, Bull."

"Easy Eddie, eh? Don't remember a name like that. When are those mine wagons due in, Charley?"

"Anytime, I guess. It's getting light fast. The switch from the mine wagons to ours should be quick." Charley Green was looking down the long street all the time he was talking with Morrison. "Jory took a quick ride around town just before you got here. A few people out and about but didn't see nothing out of the ordinary."

Morrison walked toward the corrals out behind the barns when Charley Green called to him. "Looks like we got a visitor coming, Bull. I think it's that café woman. Pushing a hand cart toward us."

"Let's sharpen up, guys. This could lead to a hit," Slim Calhoun growled. "Jory, over on the left, Charley stick with me, and Bull, cover us from back there with your rifle. Damn." Slim and Charley were deep in the shadows on one side of the barn, Jory Anderson on the other, watching Angie Whitaker push a little handcart down the street.

"I would never have thought of her being an outlaw," Calhoun muttered. "She's helped us, hates Olsen, and it looks to me like she's gonna get us off our natural guard and make us open for an ambush. Damn."

Angie put a large wicker basket together for the boys to take when they rode out later that morning. There were sourdough biscuits, cuts of smoked meat, cheeses, and coffee beans that could be ground and boiled when they stopped. She had it all in that cart she used to deliver food to people laid up from accidents in the mines.

"Good morning, Slim Calhoun," she hollered out, still twenty-five feet or so from the barn. "Brought you fellers a gift basket of good food. Hope you like smoked elk and fresh goat cheese."

"You shouldn't be here, Angie," is all Slim said, stepping out of the shadows, his pistol already in his hand. "This could get very dangerous around here. I know you think you're doing us a favor, but you could get yourself killed."

"They might want to rob you out on the trail," she smiled. "Ain't gonna rob you right in town, Slim. Come on, at least take a look at what I brought you." Her eyes were wide with charm and offered the big marshal an invitation to more than a basket of bread and cheese. In Slim's mind this had all the earmarks of a set-up, an ambush, and he had to think a long time before he answered her.

"Okay, Angie, but when we look and put the basket in the wagon you hightail it out of here. Those mine wagons are due any minute, and if we're gonna get hit, that's when it's gonna happen. Now hurry and then git." He thought she was the prettiest girl he'd seen in years, wanted to grab her up kiss her all over, and at the same time felt that all hell was about to explode around him. He had 'those feelings' again and they were seldom wrong.

Slim Calhoun could almost feel the danger that he described and did his best to move things along. "Just leave the cart, now. You can come back for it." He took the large wicker basket, and the smell of the fresh baked bread was almost too much for him. "Is this bread just out of the oven?"

"You bet, Slim. Just for you. I threw some sweet rolls in there, too. Got to keep your strength up, big boy."

"Wagons comin'," Jory Anderson yelled from the side of the barn. "Three of them comin' in fast. No outriders, just the wagons."

Slim Calhoun grabbed Angie and hustled her to the side of the barn as Charley Green joined him. "Stay where you are, Jory, until all the wagons have gone through to the corrals. Bull, you okay back there?"

"I got you boys covered. See anything else down the street?"

"Not a thing," Anderson said. He stood in the shade at the side of the barn, just inside the big open doors, rifle in hand and watched the wagons coming on fast. They were still a block and a half away and the dust they kicked up made visibility difficult but he couldn't see any movement behind the wagons. "Step back, men, they're comin' in quick."

WENDELL HARRISON WATCHED the stables from the side of his house. His horse was saddled and ready to ride when the big wagon pulled out. "What the hell?" he stammered. "What is that woman doing?" He saw Angie Whitaker come out of her café pushing that cart of hers toward the stables.

"Damn, damn, damn," he said. "No, Angie, get the hell out of there. She's sure to put a screw in this plan somehow." He saw at least one man, probably one of the marshals beckon her in and then everyone was in the shade of the barn and he couldn't see what was happening.

"Okay, here they come," he said. There was a wide smile on his face as he first heard then saw the wagons rumble through town. He felt the anticipation of having crates of gold at his bedside that night. "All that gold and Silas Houston wants to give those louts equal shares. That ain't gonna happen, Silas," he murmured. The wagons were moving fast through town, kicking up great billows of dust and debris.

"I hope everyone's where they're supposed to be. As soon as we know which road they will take, I'll ride out well behind and the rest can follow." He had what he considered a real smile on his face watching three wagons come down the street. He could feel gold coins in his pockets, see ingots in a satchel, and hear women's sighs as he walked down the streets in some little Mexican town.

Pete Olsen was enjoying the slow ascent of the sun from his perch on the boardwalk when he saw Angie step out of her café with that little pushcart of hers. "What the hell is she up to?" He wanted to yell at her, caught himself in time, and stepped into the marshal's office, out of sight.

"That woman's gonna make of mess of things, sure as hell," he muttered. There was always anger in Olsen, and it was showing through this morning. He remembered her actions at the saloon, calling him some ugly names as she tended old man Riley. "She'll pay for that," he muttered.

He was standing at the door, which was opened just enough for him to see down the street to the stables. "What is she doing?" He watched Slim Calhoun step into the light from the open barn doors and usher he in. "There's that bastard of a marshal. I should have just shot him when he walked in the door. You're dead, marshal," he said quietly. He wanted to reach down and feel the handle of his sidearm and his broken arm stopped him cold. Fear snaked its way through the angry young deputy with the knowledge that he could not face anyone. That broken arm made him a weakling for the first time in his life.

He wanted to cuss and storm down there and just shoot everybody in sight. Everybody. It was the racket of three wagons rolling quickly down the street that brought him back to reality. "Now we're getting somewhere." They rolled right on into the barns and Olsen slipped out of the office and around to the back where his horse, saddled and ready to ride, was tied off. All he had to do now was wait for the big wagon to drive off and follow it.

"I'll take my share and more if I can, but what I want more than anything is to see that marshal dead. I want him to suffer hard before he dies and I want him to know I killed him." Another thought slipped into his poisoned brain: "I wonder if he's taking Angie with him? They will die together." He was almost snarling as he moved his horse from the hitching rail to one of the side streets where he could see the barns and know which road the gold wagon would take.

"THOSE WAGONS SHOULD BE COMING down the street damn soon," Silas Houston said, standing at the door of his feed store. He could see the stables clearly and took a quick breath when he saw Angie Whitaker step out of her café, pushing her little food cart.

"What the hell is she doing?" He almost stepped out onto the boardwalk to call to her. He watched her push the cart to the barn, saw Calhoun usher her in and was about to close the door when he heard the wagons coming down the street.

"I don't know what she's doing but when that wagon full of gold pulls out of that barn, I won't have any friends with it. She's on her own if she's with it. Only marshals to die protecting my gold. Yes, it's my gold. I'm not going to offer full shares to the gunmen and especially not to that fool Pete Olsen. I've got plans no one knows about and I'll have enough gold to make 'em work."

CHAPTER NINE

"See anything?" Tiny West had sent Childers down to the corner again. "I wish we had a better view."

"Yeah, Tiny, but then the whole damn town would have a view of us, including Harrison and Houston," Jake Jackson said.

"You're right," West said. "Now, remember, boys, when those wagons ride through that barn, we've got to be right behind them, guns blazing." He was interrupted by Childers running back, hollering something. "Slow down, Childers. What is it?"

"That woman from the café is taking something to the barns. Pushing a cart over there or something. Has there been a change we don't know of?"

"Get back and watch," Tiny West said. "Wave your arms if you see those wagons. Everybody, let's get ready, those wagons have to be close." It was light enough for everything to be seen clearly even if the sun itself hadn't quite peaked over the far mountain ridge. It's always coldest just at sunrise and the crisp air had the men bundled in heavy coats.

Childers muttered some but hurried back to his corner lookout and watched Angie go into the barn. Then he heard the wagons, waved like a madman and ran toward his horse. West and the boys moved quickly toward the intersection and as the wagons roared through, fell in right behind.

SLIM CALHOUN SPOTTED the riders swing out behind the wagons and howled at the others. "Ambush," he yelled louder than the sounds of the wagons and chargers pulling them, and grabbed Angie and rolled deep into the shadows at the side of the barn, pulling that Colt as they crashed to the ground. Charley Green was right beside them, splayed out in the dirt and filth, weapon in hand.

Between support posts, wagons, and harness there was plenty of good hiding places but not necessarily good shooting places. Calhoun and Green were burrowing deep in the tangle of harness and looking for targets. "Don't move Angie," Slim yelled. She was bruised from being thrown to the ground and terrified at what was happening. She couldn't control the sobbing.

The three wagons came through the open ended

barn at a strong trot, five riders with pistols in hand right behind. Bull Morrison had a sawed-off double-barreled ten-gauge shotgun at the ready at the corral end of the barn. Those were the guns messengers carried when protecting stage coach runs.

Bull was off to the right side and noticed that Easy Eddie Martin had moved to the left side, a rifle in hand. "If he's part of this mess, he's one dead sumbitch," Morrison smiled, leveling the shotgun in Martin's direction.

He was not able to get to talk to the man before all this started and remembered that the only thing the Sierra Express Company Manager Hickson had said was there would be a teamster and a horse boy for the ride. Bull tried to watch the wagons, the men behind them, and this Easy Eddie Martin all at the same time. "Looks like many of the outlaws I've dealt with," and he chuckled just a bit, "and many of the lawmen too."

Martin gave Morrison a thumbs-up signal, turned that wicked Winchester toward the oncoming wagons and Bull settled down for a good fight. He nodded back to Easy Eddie, cocked the heavy hammers of his scattergun, and smiled ever so slightly. He'd been aching for a fight for two days.

Slim pulled down on the lead rider and drove the man right out of his saddle with two quick shots through his chest. Charley Green fired twice and Jake Jackson was flung backward off his horse. Angie was screaming in fright, first seeing Tiny West and then

Jackson killed right in front of her. She hid her tear-stained face in her hands, crying like a baby at the destruction of life.

Eddie Payson was half way out of the saddle when a bullet from Jory Anderson tore through his leg. He fell to the ground and rolled behind a bale of straw, taking a quick shot at Anderson, which missed but was close enough for Anderson to hear its whine going by. "Whooie, damn," he bellowed and dove into some straw bales.

Balderdash Emory was low on his horse's neck and riding straight for Easy Eddie Martin when the blast from Bull Morrison's shotgun took him and his horse to ground, dead. Childers jumped from his horse at the first gunshot and ducked behind whatever was available, looking for either a target to shoot or an escape hole to run through.

The wagons roared through the open doors at the back of the barn and pulled up at the corrals in a cloud of dust and debris. Angus McMurray tried to help the teamsters get their animals under control, wondering what the hell was going on in the barn. It was a melee of screaming, rearing animals, howling men, and a tornado of gunshots and screams of agony in the barns. The dust in the corrals mixed with gun smoke didn't help anyone's vision and many of the shots were just wild-chance shots.

What few people in Aurora who were awake wondered, just momentarily, what disaster was taking place this time. Only a few were out and about and they moved carefully through the town toward the stables. Gunfire always brought the lookers and in Aurora, it seemed, there was always gunfire coming from somewhere.

Eddie Payson's leg hurt like the blazes and he was working hard to get the bleeding stopped. He looked around to see who was close and saw Childers down behind some straw. He yelled, but his voice was lost in the storm of noise inside that old barn.

"Oh, no," Pete Olsen bellowed, watching the scene unfold he immediately recognized what was happening. "Those dirty bastards. So, this is how you play it, eh Mr. Houston? Change the plan after I get hurt? Ambush the wagons at the stables and cut me out? That ain't gonna happen mister."

Probably paranoid from birth, Olsen immediately blamed the ambush on Houston and was planning as quickly how to murder the man. "Have to kill him right away. Back-stabbing feed salesman tries to steal from me? He'll die right along with that marshal and Angie."

Olsen jumped on his horse and had it spurred into a full run in two steps, racing to the barns. "I'll get my fair share and kill me a marshal too," he yelled, digging his spurs deep into the horse. He saw Tiny West and Jake Jackson flung from their horses, and was almost to the barn when he saw Childers jump and tuck behind some timber. It was the horrible sound of a big shotgun that almost made him draw up.

Olsen baled off his horse just before reaching the open doors of the barn and ran to the side of the wooden door so he could see inside without being seen. It was still dark inside the barn and coupled with heavy dust thrown up, Olsen wasn't able to see anything. He crouched at the side of the door, saw Eddie Payson trying to stop the bleeding from his leg wound, and ran hard and low, diving behind a bale of straw. Two gunshots whizzed just inches from his head as he hit the ground and rolled.

Looking carefully around the bale he could see Slim Calhoun and Angie Whitaker but to get a shot he would have to show himself. He spotted Charley Green moving away from Calhoun and getting behind one of the upright timbers inside the barn, and couldn't shoot at him either. He waved his pistol and caught Childers attention, motioning him to take a couple of shots in Calhoun's direction.

"Shoot, you damn fool," he hollered. If Childers would shoot at something Olsen could move to a better hiding place. "Shoot."

"What the hell is Olsen doing here?" Childers just stared at the deputy, not understanding at all. "Has there been a change I didn't know about? Is Olsen on our side or is he acting as a deputy?" Childers didn't know whether to shoot at one of the marshals or at

Olsen. Instead, he ducked down as low as possible and did nothing.

Payson watched in disbelief as Olsen came tumbling into the barn and burrowed in the dirt behind that pillar. "I surely didn't expect this? Tiny and Jackson are dead, Childers can't hear me, and I don't know where Balderdash is. I gotta get out of here." He started crawling through the barn debris toward a stack of used harness and broken single and double trees.

"If I can make it to that trash pile I might make it to the big doors," he said. Charley Green picked up the movement and motioned to Calhoun who had a better angle.

"I got him, Charley. That was Pete Olsen who came running through the doors. I took a shot but was too late." Slim Calhoun took a long slow aim at Payson and squeezed off a single shot that hit its mark, the back of Eddie Payson's skull. "Keep an eye on where Olsen went down, Charley. He may be hurt but he's still snake dangerous."

"Oh, no," Silas Houston said. He just stood there not believing what he was watching. "What are those fools doing? What has Wendell done now?" Houston was always willing to blame Harrison for anything that might go wrong with this plan of theirs. He stood in complete awe, heard so many gunshots and then out of the corner of his eye spotted Olsen racing toward the barn.

"I've got to get down there. Something's wrong. Why is Olsen ," and he took a long breath. "Why are any of those men down there?" He walked to his horse, didn't run, and started to mount.

"No, I can't go down there. What would I do? Would I just ride right on in? What brought all this on? My God that gold was almost in my hands." He finally mounted his horse and rode toward Wendell Harrison's little shack two blocks away. "I'll get some answers or else," he muttered putting the horse in a quick trot up the hill.

Harrison was mounting his horse as Houston rode up. "What the hell's all the gunfire, Houston?"

"I was about to ask you what's going on? The gunmen along with Olsen just tried to pull off an ambush at the stables. Are you behind this, Harrison? If you are, I'm going to kill you right now," and he pulled his revolver and had it aimed at Harrison's head.

"No, Houston, no," he stammered. "What are you talking about? An ambush? At the stables? Who's behind this?"

"I thought it was you pulling a quick one on me." Houston said it quietly but didn't holster the pistol. "Why would those men do that? Why would Olsen be involved?"

There were more gunshots before Harrison could answer and the two just sat on their horses looking at each other, questions flying through their minds and not an answer coming forward.

"What should we do, Wendell?"

"Stay as far away from those stables as we can possibly get, Silas. I have a fire going, there's coffee and some good bourbon inside. Join me?"

"They have destroyed our perfect plans, Harrison. All that gold and not an ingot will be mine. If I ever see Pete Olsen or anyone of those men I will shoot them dead on sight." Silas Houston was a broken man, almost whimpering as they walked toward the little cabin.

CHILDERS SAW Payson try to sneak toward the trash pile and shook with fear when he saw his head blown apart as well. He jumped to his feet and started running toward the big doors, firing back behind him with every step. Calhoun told Charley Green to cover him and jumped to chase the man down.

Green put three shots toward where Olsen was hiding and watched Calhoun sprint through the doors. To make the shots toward Olsen he had to expose himself slightly and Olsen took quick advantage, shooting the man twice, once in the leg, and once a glancing shot to the head that didn't kill Green, but knocked him out cold.

Olsen dashed to where Green was, spotted Angie crouched with her head wrapped in her arms, sobbing.

He grabbed her and pushed her with him to the side of the barn, slowly working his way toward the doors. He was within ten feet when Calhoun came back through, holding Childers in front of him as a shield.

Bull Morrison was too far away to do anything and saw his best bet was to run as fast as he could around the outside of the barn. He motioned to Easy Eddie Martin to follow him and took off through the back doors and around to the side. "Olsen's got Angie and Slim is about to walk back into the barn. We've got to get around there now."

The two ran quickly, climbed over a high corral fence and made their way to the front of the barn, but not in time to stop Calhoun from walking through the doorway. He had tackled Childers and knocked him silly with his pistol, and forced the man to walk in front of him.

"Just keep on coming, Marshal," Olsen said, holding Angie in front of him. "Right on through those doors. One little mistake and this little whore dies."

"Easy does it, Mr. Olsen." Calhoun saw Olsen stiffen at the slight and continued, using an almost soft, quiet tone. "All your compadres are dead and there's nowhere for you to run. You're already hurt, mister. Let the lady go and you'll live to see another day. There are three other marshals just behind you, Olsen, and at least one of them is a sharp-shooter."

"Drop your gun, Marshal. Drop it." Olsen said, quickly putting the barrel of his revolver to Angie's head. It was cocked and Slim could see Olsen's finger on the trigger. Angie's eyes were huge, with horror and fright, and Slim saw that Olsen was holding his gun in his left hand, and holding Angie with his broken arm.

"Those men behind you aren't going to wait much longer, mister." Calhoun could see Jory Anderson moving slowly through the shadows getting in position for a clean kill and wondered where Bull Morrison was. Morrison was deadly with a sidearm and remembered he had been carrying that monster shotgun of his.

"You ease yourself inside, Marshal, nice and slow. To the side and we'll step out of the barn. One wrong move and she's dead." Olsen knew the marshal hadn't dropped his weapon and knew he couldn't kill Angie either. He needed her and knew Calhoun needed Childers.

Anger and frustration were taking their toll on the man's thinking capabilities as well. "Why did they try this ambush? Where were Houston and Harrison? Why wasn't he told?" Questions turned to hatred. He needed to kill somebody and the only questions were who and when. Somebody had to be blamed for all this. Paranoia demanded that somebody had to take the blame. It was always easier to blame whoever was closest at the time.

Olsen's eyes narrowed to slits and he watched Calhoun take a step to his left and he took a couple to his right. Like a dance, they exchanged positions at the barn door's opening.

Now inside the barn, Calhoun could see a few townspeople gathered at buildings and street corners waiting for the blood to flow. He kept Childers in front of him, kept that Colt ready to either blow Childers' head off or kill Olsen. "Where the hell is Morrison," he murmured, trying to see some kind of movement out behind the injured deputy city marshal.

Angie was crying even harder as Olsen pulled her out of the barn and was slowly backing his way to his horse. "Shut up, woman. You'll die just as soon as we're out of town. Shut up," he snarled. She struggled and he had a hard time holding her because of his bad arm and finally swatted her across the side of her head.

At that moment Bull Morrison swung the shotgun and slammed Pete Olsen across the side of his head with some heavy metal, dropping the man instantly. "I wondered where you were," Calhoun said, stepping out of the barn with Childers. "I appreciate your timely help."

"Seems like I spend a great deal of time saving your life, Slim Calhoun."

Angie jumped free of Olsen as he crumpled to the ground and flung herself at Calhoun. "Oh, Slim, thank God you got here. You saved me, Slim. Oh, God," and she fainted dead away, in his arms. Morrison scowled and Calhoun smiled.

Easy Eddie grabbed Childers and held him tight

and Morrison got Olsen back on his feet. "These are some rather stupid people you're dealing with, Marshal," Martin said with a quick smile. "If I had plans to steal a shipment like we're taking north, I think I would have done it out on the road somewhere."

"Stupid is another way of spelling outlaw, Easy Eddie," Slim Calhoun said. "Where's Charley?" He sprinted back into the barn and found the deputy just coming to, with blood pouring from a crease across his head, just above his left eye, and more blood oozing from his leg.

Calhoun hollered back to Morrison. "Charley's taking a nap, damn his hide. Always thinking of himself." He eased the big man to a sitting position and used Charley's shirt to wipe away some of the blood and get the flow stopped. "You don't want it to ever get any closer to the golden staircase than this, Charley Green." Green was holding the bandage in place and Slim helped him to his feet.

"Looks like I missed most of the action, eh?" He chuckled. "I like it that way but this is gonna hurt like hell tomorrow." Two quick shots interrupted anything else Green might have wanted to say.

CHAPTER TEN

ANGIE WAS CLINGING TO EASY EDDIE MARTIN AS Pete Olsen slowly came out of his fog. Olsen's head was bleeding from the whack he took and he watched Calhoun walk into the barn. Morrison was holding Olsen's broken arm with one hand and held that shotgun with the other. Olsen took the extra couple of minutes to get his head on straight, primed himself and made a grab for Morrison's sidearm, wrenching his broken arm free of the man's grip.

Pain from the broken arm almost ruined the play, but he grabbed the pistol, spun free, and rolled onto the ground. He fired two quick shots at Morrison, got to his feet and sprinted to his horse, which was still tied just fifteen feet away. During the melee the cast was broken and the pain almost caused the man to pass out. He fought off the nausea, stumbled and almost fell. Olsen's pain stabbed hard when he tried to mount, finally climbed in the saddle, and rode hard right up the main street of Aurora.

Between Angie's death grip and Martin trying to hold Childers, he couldn't get free, finally pushing her away. By the time he got the rifle up he didn't have a shot and stood watching the desperate deputy race down the main street, which was almost crowded with onlookers. "Too many people," he muttered in disgust.

Calhoun ran from the barn in time to see Olsen ride off and ran to Morrison's side. Bull was bent over in pain and Calhoun eased him to the ground getting some strong language from the senior marshal. "Where'd he get you, Bull?"

"If you laugh I'll shoot you," Morrison grumbled. "Right in my butt."

"Well, can't do no harm there. I'm going after that fool. Get yourself and Charley patched up and get that wagon on the road. Take Jory with you, he's not much good on a chase." Calhoun and Morrison had been partners long enough that Calhoun often took the lead during times of action.

"I'll need Easy Eddie too," Morrison said. "Don't go alone, Slim. That ain't good."

"No, I'm taking Angus McMurray. He knows this area like nobody else. Get that gold to Carson City, Bull."

"I'll take care of everybody," Angie said. "I've never been so afraid in all my life. I'm okay now, though. You kill that Pete Olsen, Slim Calhoun. You kill him." She helped Morrison to his feet and the bunch of them walked into the barn. Calhoun couldn't hold back the chuckles watching Morrison and his bloody rear end disappear into the barn.

"They're a real mess, they are." Bull's bloody backside, Green's bloody head and leg, and Angie's bloody head had Calhoun standing in the barn doorway shaking his head and trying to hold back the chuckles.

"THAT'S THE SITUATION, Angus. Will you ride with me? I won't ask you to get into a gunfight or anything like that, but I need a good guide. Olsen knows this country and so do you. Will you scout for me?"

"There ain't nothin' I'd rather do, Marshal. We'll separate that basket of food Angie brought and put it in our saddlebags, and be out of here in less than five minutes." He was already saddling a fine looking stud and Calhoun was fetching the basket.

It was chaos in the corrals. The horse boy and Easy Eddie working to get the horses and wagon connected, Morrison yelling at Anderson to keep a close look-out for more danger, Angie working over Charley Green, and Calhoun and McMurray getting mounted for the chase.

Those two rode out of the barn within six minutes, actually, according to the report that Bull Morrison filed later. When a bit of calm was restored, Angie had Morrison off to the side with his pants down around his knees, cleaning the bullet wound in his generous butt. "One word lady and I'll shoot you just like I would have shot Slim."

She just giggled and poured some of Angus McMurray's fine bourbon in the wound, which brought a howl of pain from the marshal. "You did that on purpose," Bull yelled loud enough to be heard out on the street.

Angie smiled and said, "Of course I did." She fashioned a bandage for the wound and Morrison got his pants up where they belonged. "There now, that'll fix you up just fine. Let's take a look at that head of yours, Charley."

"While she's fixin' Charley, gather 'round, Anderson and Easy Eddie, we've got some plannin' to do." Morrison was working hard to get his dignity back and watched Anderson and Martin stifle the chuckles. "That gold shipment is sitting back there with just the horse boy watching it. Jory, you hustle out there and keep a close eye. Martin, you were supposed to be our teamster, so finish up whatever needs to be done harnessing and we've got to get on the road."

Bull Morrison stood up arranged the bandage on his behind and tightened his pants up just as a tall thin man walked into the barn wearing a badge on his fine frock coat. He had light gray eyes and blondish hair and gave the impression that he'd never done a lick of hard work in his life.

"What's going on here?" he demanded.

"Who wants to know?" Bull Morrison chortled. He was buckling his gunbelt back in place.

"I'm Aurora City Marshal Wilson. What's all the gunfire? Who are you men?"

"Nice of you to show up, Mr. Wilson, even if you are late for the party. Jory, Eddie, hop to it. I need to speak a few hundred words with this dandy." He motioned Conrad Wilson to follow him and walked into McMurray's little office near the front of the barn. *This feller looks more like a transient gambler than a lawman.* Morrison was angry enough that he might just shoot somebody because he could.

He slammed the office door and spun on the city marshal, eyes blazing and fists knotted for war. "Your so-called deputy just tried to rob the gold shipment scheduled out of town this morning. In the process several people have died, others have been wounded, and Mr. Olsen is attempting to evade my deputy." He shoved the marshal into McMurray's chair by the desk.

"Just who are you?" Wilson didn't even know U.S. Marshals were in his town. He made an attempt to get back on his feet and Morrison punched him in the middle of his chest knocking him back down.

"I'm your worst dream right now, Wilson." Morrison bent over, his face just inches from Wilson's. "I'm U.S. Marshal Bull Morrison here to escort that gold that your deputy attempted to steal." Morrison stood up and walked to the wood stove and poured a cup of hot coffee. He didn't offer any to Wilson.

Instead he placed his hand gently on his pistol. "Was he working on your orders? Because if I find out he was, you won't have time for a trial. There ain't nothin' in the world lower than a lawman goin' bad." Morrison had a firm grip on that heavy revolver but it was still in its leather.

When Bull Morrison's anger reached a certain level that ugly scar running across his face turned almost scarlet, his eyes became glowing coals, and his lips became thin and white. Conrad Wilson watched Morrison's jaws tighten, saw those horrible eyes and that ugly scar, and wanted to run from the office. His whole body was shaking in fear and he couldn't take his eyes off Morrison's face, those eyes, that massive scar.

Conrad Wilson was a frail man, a politician, not a real city marshal. "What are you talking about?" He stammered. "I was just elected two days ago. Just took office yesterday. No, Marshal Morrison. No." Perspiration dripped from his ash white face, sheer terror shone in his light eyes, and his hands were shaking like aspen leaves in the fall. Wilson was still crumpled into a chair near McMurray's desk, almost whimpering in fear.

"Don't think I've ever seen a man wearing a badge cry like a baby," Morrison grumbled. "My deputy, Slim Calhoun is chasing Pete Olsen right now, Wilson. Where is Olsen likely to run to? Come on man, grow up. Where would Olsen run?"

"I don't know," Wilson whimpered. Morrison

pulled his revolver and opened the trap to check for loads, snapped it shut, and cocked the hammer. "No, Marshal. I don't know. I don't even hardly know Olsen. He came with the job."

"I'm giving you another job right now," Morrison said. "That man there, the one that's all tied up and bruised and bloody is my prisoner. You put him in your jail and when I get this gold delivered to Carson City I'll be back. If my prisoner isn't in your jail, all safe and sound, I'll kill you three times. Got it?" He slowly brought the pistol up, took carful aim at a point between Wilson's eyes, and watched the man wet his pants.

Morrison couldn't help smiling, put the pistol back in its leather, and said, in a quiet voice, "Go play politician somewhere, Wilson. If I find out you're involved, I'll shoot you twice. And remember what I said about my prisoner. Get out." He was still chuckling when he walked back to where Angie was working on Charley Green.

"Can you travel, Charley? We gotta get this gold out of this town."

"He doesn't even know who he is, Marshal," Angie said. "That bullet knocked him silly. He needs to spend several days in bed. I can take care of him, but he sure can't ride a horse or wagon."

"All right, then, let's get him to your place. I've got to get this wagon moving before some other bunch of stupid people decide to try and take that gold." They got Charley on his wobbly feet and off to the little apartment Angie had next door to her café.

Charley Green was in a large bed in a second bedroom. "I hope you can hear me, Charley," Morrison said, and saw the man nod just a bit. "Good. When you are able to move, help Slim if you can, and try to see who was behind all this. That idiot of a town marshal is holding one of the outlaws for us. See to it that he's kept safe. We'll get that gold delivered and get back here pronto.

"We'll be gone, hell, ten days or more and Slim's gonna need help. I want to know who is behind this." Green nodded even if his eyes didn't seem to be focused. He reached out and grabbed Morrison's arm and gave it a squeeze and another nod.

"Get him well, Angie. I need him," Morrison said. Bull rushed back to the barn and got the little armada underway. "Two men short ain't gonna make for a good trip." Easy Eddie was driving the teams with the horse boy alongside him, and Jory Anderson and Bull Morrsion trailed. "Take the point, Jory and I'll trail for the first couple of hours, then we'll switch. Keep your eyes open wide. Those fools may have help."

The sun was well above the rim of those mountains as the caravan moved out of Aurora. "We're already two, maybe three hours behind time, visible to the whole damn world, and two men short. If there's anything else gonna go wrong, it better understand just how riled I am," Bull Morrison muttered, nudging his horse a bit. High, dazzling white clouds dotted a brilliant blue sky and warm air drifted down the side of the mountain offering a gentle late summer morning's foray into the great Nevada wilderness.

OLSEN RODE FAST for a full hour leaving Aurora on a single track to the south, hoping to get far enough that he could turn into a rocky canyon that led high into the mountains to the east. He could think of nothing but getting away, but other thoughts slowly crept back into his warped mind. Things like killing Angie for being nice to the marshal. Killing the marshal for embarrassing him, showing no respect for who he was, and for being responsible for his broken arm.

Thoughts about why Houston and Harrison had changed the plan and attacked the marshals at the stables slowly worked their way through his anger and paranoia settled in. "They must have put this together to keep me from getting my share of that gold. It was Harrison behind this," he grumbled.

His plan was to find a good spot to set up a solid camp, wait several days, and slip back into Aurora and kill Harrison, Houston, and Angie Whitaker. He knew these mountains, canyons, water sources well having hunted the area for several years. He knew of several spots that would make good hideouts and one that would be best.

The trail led down to where a steep canyon,

narrow and rocky, wound its way through willows, crossing a small stream many times and ending up in a high, broad meadow. He dropped off the trail and made his way up that canyon, crossing and re-crossing the little creek. It was a long slow ride and the day was starting to peter out by the time he reached the meadow. He rode northeast across the rocky plain and up into towering rocks, finding a little grotto where he could make camp. Pines and spruce, aspen and cedar grew where the rocks let them, grasses came in small bunches, and Olsen found the little fire pit just as he'd left it last time he was there.

The only thing tied to the back of his horse was a slicker and a bedroll. He did have some trail food and some coffee in his saddlebags, since he was planning to be somewhere that evening counting out hundreds of gold coins. He put together a quick fire, gathered more wood, and had coffee going before laying out his bedroll. "I'll spend a few days here, duck back into town and pick up what I need, kill those double-crossing bastards, and clear out of this country." He sat back on his heels with a sly grin. "What I need is gold. And that bank has some."

He opened a can of beans and thought more about that. "I need to kill those people that ruined this plan and I need gold. Should I rob the bank and then kill them or the other way around." He was almost laughing when he threw the empty can away. "If anyone tried to follow me out of town they can't follow me through all those rocks and up that canyon."

He opened a bottle of whiskey he had in the saddlebags. He planned on toasting a successful hit on the mint wagon with that whiskey, not successfully fleeing a mangled attempt at an ambush. Between the pain of his broken arm and hot whiskey, Olsen was asleep just as the sun fell behind the western mountains.

"HE SURE AIN'T TRYING to hide his trail, Angus. You sure this is his horse we're trackin'?"

"Oh, yeah," McMurray chuckled. "Gotta remember, Slim, I'm the blacksmith what shod that pony. We're following Pete Olsen. Watch to the sides if we get into rocky country just in case he gets off this track he's on. It leads into some high country and there are many deep canyons with creeks that we'll pass. You'll find canyons with creeks about every three to five miles along this valley.

"This country is where many of the boys come to shoot deer and mountain sheep. Many of the canyons lead up to high mountain meadows. When we pass one of those creeks, watch for tracks leading off this trail."

"He gained a lot of time on us," Calhoun said. "He's been pushing that horse hard all day, too. I expect he'll be looking to cozy up before too long."

The ride through the thin high mountain air, the

aroma of pine, cedar, and spruce, and the shear beauty of the alpine scenes weren't lost on Slim Calhoun. "It's a shame we're chasing a killer, Angus. We should have pack mules and supplies for two weeks with plans for a nice hunt. You live mighty close to heaven, my friend."

McMurray smiled at the thought, gazing up at towering peaks that soared well over the ten thousand foot mark. Far across the valley he could see the ragged spires of the Sierra Nevada, most still covered in last winter's snow. He spread his arms wide and remembered his boyhood in the mountains of Scotland. "Aw, Laddie-buck, I hear a poet singing those words. Yes, I see that beauty, and feel the music of these mountains, Slim. Aye, my friend, this could be heaven if it weren't for the man we're looking for."

The conversation came to an abrupt end when Slim spotted hoof prints leading off the trail and following a small stream up into a deep and dark canyon. "Looks like we'll be making camp somewhere up this canyon, Angus."

CHAPTER ELEVEN

"I watched that wagon pull right out of the stables and straight down the trail. They took the road that would connect with the Walker River Road, Silas. Just like we thought they would." Wendell Harrison seemed like a broken man when he walked into the restaurant at the Borealis Hotel and joined Silas Houston for breakfast. "There were only two marshals riding guard and that nasty teamster, Easy Eddie Martin driving.

"What went wrong, Silas? We had it so well planned out. All we had to do was follow that wagon."

"I think Pete Olsen went wrong, Wendell. I think he convinced those others to ambush the wagon at the stables and he did it all wrong. I was able to watch some of it and Olsen arrived late. That would be his arrogant way, you know. And the others were simply outgunned. They were cut down riding into the barn, as if the marshals were waiting for them."

The mining man was just as sure as the feed store owner that it was Olsen who changed the plan. "If I ever see that man again, I'll shoot him dead," Harrison said. "First, killing that one man and wounding another. Old men who couldn't fight back, and then getting his arm broke trying to be a big man with a federal marshal. We picked the wrong man, Silas and I'm worried now about us. What do we do now? Sure as all get-out fingers will be pointed our way."

"Why? Who knows we're involved in any of this?" He sat back with a smug smile on his face. "We've done everything we could to keep out of sight on this. We just picked the wrong person to be the third member."

"For one, Brady Throckmorton. For two, Childers. Childers is sitting in that jail right over there," and he nodded to the marshal's office across the street from the hotel. "Childers will tell that new marshal everything. One good punch to the nuts and Throckmorton will scream out our names. We've got to do something, Silas."

"Let's not talk about it here." The dining room was filling fast and there were lots of ears. "Let's go up to that warehouse of mine. It's quiet, there won't be anyone around to accidentally hear something. You're right, though, whatever we decide has to be done as soon as possible. Do you think Olsen will get away?"

"I saw Angus McMurray ride out with that impudent marshal. I doubt if they'll capture him. They'll bring him back slung across a saddle."

"I hope so. He plays tough but he'd talk if that marshal started pounding on him. We would have been better off picking anyone else for his part."

"Maybe. Remember we picked that fool because of his gun and his badge, neither one of which had a damn thing to do with yesterday. All that gold," Harrison almost wept, "gone. Just gone."

"WELL, NOW," Angie Whitaker exclaimed coming into Charley Green's bedroom and finding him fastening his shirt. "Just look at you. Are you sure you're feeling well enough to be up and about? You took one big bump to that pretty head of yours."

"It's your nursin', Angie. I've got a roaring headache and my leg hurts like the devil, but I've got to get over to that jail." He wore a bloody bandage wrapped around his head and if one looked carefully, there was a bandage stuffed in the right leg of his pants, probably bloody as well.

"Well, Mr. Marshal, sir, you ain't goin' nowhere until you eat something. I gotta get back to my café, so you come over as soon as you're finished dressin'. Food first, mister." She was smiling, flirting actually, and Charley bowed slightly, grabbed her hand and gave it a little kiss.

"Yes, ma'am. I'll do as you say, but it was a deputy

city marshal in on that attempted robbery yesterday. Is the city marshal himself in on the plot? And if he is, he's holding one of the gang members in his jail. I can't waste too much time, here."

"You just get to the café right away. Johnnycakes, side meat, and some eggs all whipped up. If you're gonna be out there playing marshal you're gonna want some good food to keep you big and strong." She had a wicked smile on her face and Charley couldn't help blushing just a bit, which of course simply gave her full satisfaction. "Want some chilies in them eggs?" She teased some more.

"That would be just fine." He was stammering and smiling as he pulled his boots on, strapped his big colt around his waist, and followed Angie out the door. "Nice living right next door to your business. How long you been in Aurora?"

"Been here two years, but only had the café for a year. Worked in the hotel the first year, and that weren't no fun a'tall. You been a marshal for a long time?"

"Goin' on five years, now. Been with Bull and Slim the last two. They are a pair to ride with."

"I'd like to ride with Slim," she murmured. Green was still blushing when she poured his coffee. She fixed enough food to sink a Missouri steamer and Charley Green headed for the marshal's office and jail. "Been in this town two years, hundreds of single men minin' gold, and she ain't married yet." He was muttering when he opened the door and met Conrad Wilson. "I ain't never met a woman like her." He walked into the sparse office of the city marshal and found Wilson sitting at his desk lighting a cigar.

"Mornin'," Green said. "I'm Deputy U.S. Marshal Charley Green. You Wilson?"

"I am Aurora City Marshal Conrad Wilson," he said, as if correcting Green. "What do you want?" He didn't stand and offer a hand or a cup of coffee, just a scowl.

"Just checking on our prisoner and want a conversation with the man." He found an old chair by the wall and dragged it over in front of the desk. He glanced at the stove with the coffee pot on top and decided against it. "And a conversation with you. How is it your deputy was involved in that attempted robbery yesterday? Most unusual, don't you think?"

"Don't know enough about the man to say anything," Wilson grumped. "You got a badge or something? How do I know you're a marshal?"

Charley chuckled and remembered that they weren't wearing their badges. "You're trying to be a rough old codger, Wilson. It ain't in you, pard." Green pulled his badge out of a pocket and showed it to Wilson. He pinned the badge on proper, walked to the wood stove and poured a cup of coffee into a tin cup sitting on a shelf. "Now you know I am one," he snickered.

"That all you're gonna say about this Pete Olsen.

He's your deputy and people died yesterday because he was involved in an illegal activity. Two U.S. Marshals were wounded, me being one of them." He allowed just a hint of anger to show through. "You're sitting there acting like you're not the least bit interested and that ain't how a lawman should be. Do you understand what I said? People are dead and injured because of one of your deputies.

"You better talk straight with me, Aurora City Marshal Conrad Wilson or you might find yourself tucked away in your own little jail back there. We were sent here to escort a large load of gold to the U.S. Mint in Carson City and were attacked by your deputy, who is now on the run being followed by one of our deputies."

Charley Green had a reputation within the service of getting answers when no one else was able to. He had an evil smile on his face when he mentioned putting the marshal in a cell in his own jail. "These aren't hard questions, Wilson. Are you or are you not involved in this attempted robbery of gold owned by the government of the United States?"

Conrad Wilson wasn't prepared for an attack such as this and sat with a dumb look on his face for several seconds. He wasn't a big man to start with, depended on his ability to manipulate people, to find some way to play one against the other, and had never come up against anyone like the deputy marshal.

"Now, just a minute, Marshal. Just calm down,

please. I was just elected a few days ago and this Pete Olsen came with the job. I know the man has a bad reputation around town, so did the former marshal whom I soundly defeated at the polls.

"I talked with Ted Hickson at the express office yesterday and he said that Ed Montgomery, the former city marshal, was informed of you folks coming and of the shipment, but I didn't know anything about any of it until I heard those gunshots. If Olsen is involved then he needs to be caught and brought to trial." Wilson was talking fast, almost pleading, his hands in front of him, palms up. He won the election and now he's threatened with being put in his own jail. How did it come to this, he wondered.

Green sipped some coffee and pondered on what Wilson said. "I'm takin' you at your word, Wilson, but the fires of hades will lick your heels if you're lyin' to me. You plannin' on putting a posse together to find this deputy of yours?"

Wilson just sat in his old chair with a dumb look on his face. It was several seconds before Charley Green just chuckled at the stupidity he was working with. "Where's Childers, I need to talk to him?"

Wilson stood up slowly and led Green to the back of the building where the cells were. Childers was bruised and scratched some but not seriously injured. "You got yourself a whole trainload of trouble, Childers. You got a first name?"

"Alphonse," he said. He was sitting on the edge of a

straw filled mattress in the six-foot by eight-foot cell. "Who are you?"

"I'm one of the good guys that you tried to kill yesterday. Who were you working for, Pete Olsen?"

"P'shaw. Pete wasn't even supposed to be there," and he shut up quickly. Childers wasn't quick on mind matters and wondered why this marshal thought Pete was the boss. He wondered if this man knew about Houston and Harrison.

"No? He surely was, though. Did you really think you could ambush four federal marshals inside a barn? Who put you up to this, Alphonse Childers? Tell me whose plan this was and maybe I can make it a little easier for you."

"You mean the ambush plan?" Childers didn't know which plan the marshal was talking about. A light went on in Green's mind too. He now had to wonder about two plans. Were they by the same people?

"Well," Childers continued, "we thought the plan to ambush the wagons on the road to Carson City was a good one, but it was Tiny West thought we should hit the gold shipment right at the stables."

Things started to come clear to Charley Green. "I'll be back and we'll talk some more, Childers. Don't go anywhere," he chuckled, rattling the cell bars some. *My goodness,* he thought. *Plans were made by someone to attack the wagon on the road and then one of the outlaws changed the plan. That means that whoever made the first plan wasn't at the barn.*

He said Olsen wasn't supposed to be there. Was it his plan that was changed? Or had he been cut out of the deal? Maybe because of the broken ar? His thoughts were rambling around his head fast and he needed to go somewhere quiet, think hard, and make plans of his own. He was shaking his head as he walked out of the cell area and into Wilson's office. The man still sitting at his desk.

"When Pete Olsen killed Roddy Simpson and shot Ed Riley the other night, why didn't you arrest him?"

"He said the men accosted him. I believed him." Wilson's smug attitude was returning.

"Those men were stove up retired miners who couldn't possibly accost a tit mouse, Wilson, more or less a young man like Olsen. You shame that badge you're wearing. You keep my prisoner, Childers alive. You hear me?" he shouted. "Somebody in this town was behind that attack and he knows who. They will come looking for him. You got me?" Green was more than ready to shoot Wilson, thought that Bull Morrison would probably already have done so, and glared at the city marshal.

"He's safe here," is all Wilson said, turning from Charley Green. Green smiled at the insolence and strolled out the door knowing that Childers' days might very well be numbered. "I think a long cup of coffee in a quiet little café will do me some good right about now. If anyone knows who might be behind this screwed up attack it's that little darlin' Angie." He was muttering all the way down the street. "Probably more than one making the plans and probably well known in town."

"AIN'T no kind of morning to be trackin' some damn fool outlaw, McMurray." Slim Calhoun had a fire going with coffee boiling when the sun peaked over a high ridge. They were deep in a narrow canyon next to a creek that promised fresh cold water. "We should be fishing for trout or hunting deer, not lookin' to kill a man."

"That meadow I told you about is less than a mile in front of us, Slim. There are a hundred places up there where he could be hiding. My thought is we go high from here, on foot, and take a good look at that meadow. It's probably about a hundred acres across with the stream boiling down the center."

"You're afraid we'd give ourselves away riding the horses up there? Yeah, I think you're right. Let's see if we can surprise the jerk."

They finished their coffee and worked their way up the side of the canyon, then followed the ridge toward the meadow. They were actually above the broad plain when it came into sight and were well hidden in a stand of tall pines, fir, and spruce with a good view of the grassy meadow. The stream had willows in places and stands of aspen stood tall in the open air. There were groves of ubiquitous cottonwood trees as well.

"That's a beautiful sight, Angus. That sparkling little creek's got to have trout just itchin' to be in our pan. I do believe I just saw a little wisp of smoke across over there," Slim Calhoun said. "See it?" He was pointing at some heavy timber up some and off the edge of the meadow.

"Looks like our man doesn't think he's being followed, Slim. It might take a couple of hours but if we stay in these trees we can be there without him knowing it."

"Like I said yesterday, Angus. It's my duty to bring him in. All I asked for was a guide, a tracker, and you've done just as I asked. You don't have to get any more involved. It could get a little dangerous." He chuckled and patted McMurray on the shoulder.

"A little?" McMurray laughed. "As I said yesterday, I'm with you. That bastard attacked my stables, Slim. I don't much care for that." They were smiling and chuckling as they started off through the trees on the long trek around that high alpine meadow. "Besides, I never did like that smart-mouthed kid and his swagger."

"I don't want to shoot him unless I absolutely have to. Just back my play, Angus. He's a hothead, quick to go for his gun, and not very smart. Hopefully we'll catch him with his pants down."

CHAPTER TWELVE

Pete Olsen slept with dreams of lost gold, of friends stabbing him in the back, of Angie Whitaker laughing at him as he stood on a scaffold with a rope around his neck. He was in a foul mood when he rolled out of his bedding and got a fire going. He kicked rocks because he could, burned his biscuits, and tried to drink the coffee before blowing on it.

Olsen was not the sort to make a good camp. His gear was spread out in no kind of order, his fire pit was sloppy and the wood he brought in was in every possible length. His attitude toward life was obvious.

He saw the sun spread its glow across the meadow, saw sparkling diamonds dance on the creek's waters, and cursed everything and everyone. "I should be counting hundreds of little squares of gold right now." He wanted to scream his anger, kill something, anything. There were plans to be made and that meant he had to calm down, to think, to work out something.

He spent his first hour of the morning gathering wood enough for two or three days, seeing to it that his horse was hobbled in deep grass, and creating various ways for Silas Houston and Wendell Harrison to die. He already knew how he was going to kill Angie. Long and slow with a knife. A shot to the head was too good for her.

He was stooped over the fire, reaching for the coffee pot when he heard what was surely a footstep in the brush. He raced to some large boulders near his bedroll and dove to the ground.

"Who's there?" He shouted at the brush, at the trees surrounding his camp. He fell still, listening for the slightest sound, searching for the least movement. His revolver was cocked and held firmly in his left hand, waiting for some movement. No sound, no movement, just the slightest breeze giving the branches and trees an opportunity to practice their dancing.

There hasn't been Indian trouble in these parts for some time, he thought, and he was sure that no one had followed. *Too many rocks to follow my trail and besides that I rode through the meadow in the middle of the creek.*

After at least five minutes he slowly stood up, his pistol still in hand, cocked and ready, and moved back to the fire. He slipped the revolver into its holster and with shaking hands got a cup of coffee poured. He raised the cup and was about to take a sip when a bullet smashed through the cup splashing boiling coffee into his face.

Olsen, crying in pain, rolled to the side drawing his weapon and firing it twice at where he thought the bullet came from. He couldn't see and the pain seared through him. He was about to shoot again when something crashed into the side of his head and he went down, out like a lantern in a gale.

Slim Calhoun grabbed Olsen's weapon before the man hit the ground. "Angus, are you okay? Angus, say something." Calhoun thought he heard a groan when Olsen fired at them and now heard a slight moan again. He raced back to where the men had hidden in thick brush finding the blacksmith writhing in pain, blood streaming from one of his legs.

"My God, man. Let's get you by the fire and get that bleeding stopped." He helped the big man to his feet and they stumbled into Olsen's camp. Calhoun used his knife to rip the pants leg right off McMurray. "That bullet cut right on through your tough old hide, Angus." He wrapped the rags tight and tied them off, stemming the flow.eHHHhhhhhhhjjkfks "There, that should hold your blood inside where it belongs. Didn't hit a vein or nothing. Let me get this ignorant fool tied up and then we'll clean that wound good." The wound was far more serious than Calhoun would let on. He was sure the bone had been nicked and wasn't at sure whether the bleeding was really under control. He also felt the fear of infection before he could get the man to medical help. They were a long way from town and now with a criminal in custody.

"You must live a good life, sir," he chuckled. Calhoun recognized the serious position this put them in and wanted to keep McMurray in the best of spirits. A dangerous killer as a prisoner and a wounded back up with little or no lawman background, miles from any kind of help was not how he wanted this to end. "I'm gonna fix you up just fine."

"That's good, Slim. Strange that it doesn't hurt."

"It will," Calhoun chuckled. "Give it time and it'll hurt like hell. Did you by any chance put that bottle of bourbon in your saddlebags?"

"Yes, yes," he said quickly. "Oh, my, I could surely go for a nice little nip right now."

"I was thinking along the lines of cleanin' the wound," he chuckled. Slim Calhoun pulled a length of rope from Olsen's saddle and tied the outlaw tight to a tree, made sure Angus knew that he would have to shoot Olsen should he break loose, and headed at a fast walk across the meadow back to where the horses were hobbled. "Be back quick as I can, Angus. Shoot the bastard if he gives you any trouble."

"I might not wait for him to start something," McMurray said, trying his best to laugh just a bit. He sat near the fire, his back to a cottonwood log, cradling his rifle.

THE PAIN BECAME intense about half an hour after Calhoun left and McMurray was also feeling weak from the loss of blood. That was about when Pete Olsen became aware of being tied to a tree. Olsen slowly opened his eyes, grimaced with pain from the blow to his head, and let his eyes focus. His broken arm was twisted behind his back and the pain brought tears to his eyes. He saw Angus McMurray sitting on the ground, one leg stretched out and covered with a bloody bandage.

McMurray had a rifle cradled across his lap and held a cup of coffee. McMurray saw a flicker of movement from Olsen and stiffened slightly. Olsen's head was a bloody mess from the whack by the rifle barrel, his arm was twisted and cock-eyed in that broken cast, and his face was bright red from the effects of splashing hot coffee. McMurray could see that the deputy's eyes were open.

"Waking up, are you," he said. "Good, 'cuz I never ever wanted to shoot a man what was asleep. Be stupid with me, Olsen, and I'll shoot you dead."

"What the hell are you doing here, old man? Untie me. Do you remember who I am? Untie me." He was screaming, not pleading, thrashing about, and Angus McMurray had to laugh at the pitiful sight.

"Yeah, Olsen, I know who you are. You are the outlaw who tried to rob the U.S. Mint shipment. You are the outlaw responsible for a couple or more people being dead. You are the outlaw that I'm going to help bring to the gallows. Any other questions, Mr. Outlaw?"

Olsen was in a rage, fighting the ropes, kicking his tied heels into the dirt, squirming like a pig in the mud, and screaming obscenities. "I'll kill you, McMurray. I'll kill you." He spent a full five minutes furiously fighting the ropes, ripping flesh from his arms and legs in the process. He finally weakened and slumped against the ropes, sucking in air.

"Glad you got that out of your system." McMurray's pain was fierce and he wasn't going to let Olsen know that. *I hope Slim can get back with those horses soon. I'm not sure I can stay awake much longer.* Blood loss and shock were taking their toll and McMurray wasn't a young man either. McMurray's background was all about horses, mules, and caring for them. He helped the local militia with their animals and that was the extent of his knowledge of military, and he had no knowledge of what a lawman would do in this situation.

Olsen watched as Angus McMurray slowly slipped into a peaceful sleep and started working on getting unbound. All the flailing around stretched the ropes some but they were also bloody and slick. His hands were behind him and tied around a limb of a small spruce bush. He strained as hard as he could and then tried to slip out of the rope and couldn't.

He worked at getting his hands free for a full hour and could feel that he was making a little progress.

Even if he could get one hand free it would help. McMurray hadn't moved in that time and Olsen didn't know if anyone else might be around somewhere. He felt his hand slip slowly out of one loop of rope and took a deep breath before working on the other hand.

"Just a little bit more," he muttered. "Come on, slip out." He had ripped skin from his wrists to the point that even a slight amount of movement sent shocks of pain up his arm. Incredible pain brought tears to the man's eyes as he wrenched hard and felt his hand come free of the rope. Olsen was having a hard time breathing from the pain in his hands, from the blow to his head, and from the extreme amount of energy he had used getting free. He had done more damage to the broken cast on his arm and could actually hear the ends of the broken bones scrape together.

He had to take a short rest, had to catch his breath, before he tackled getting his feet untied. He saw McMurray move slightly and knew he couldn't rest, couldn't stop. Just another few minutes and he'd be free, free to kill McMurray and get on his horse and ride away.

"How did he find me? Why is the blacksmith chasing me? Where is his horse?" He was looking all around his little camp and couldn't understand what had happened. He muttered more and more questions, all without answers, as he worked to get the ropes off his legs and never heard the hooves of two horses slowly move into the area.

"Looks like I better practice my knot tying, eh?" Slim walked the two horses to where Olsen's was tethered and tied them off. "You're a mess, Mr. Olsen, and furthermore, you're under arrest, which means if you piss me off I will be fully justified in shooting you dead." He reached in his saddlebags and pulled a set of handcuffs out. "Let's check these for size, shall we?"

Olsen's wrists were bloody, the skin torn away from the wrenching and twisting in the rope, and when Calhoun pulled his arms back around him and fastened the cuffs Olsen couldn't hold back the moans of pain. "By golly that broken arm sure does bend easy, eh? Now let's see what we can do for our fine blacksmith. Angus, can you hear me? We got to get you back to Aurora and let a doc take care of you."

McMurray stirred a bit but didn't say anything while Calhoun slipped the bloody bandage off the wound. "At least the bullet went all the way through, old man. This is gonna hurt," he said. The Kentucky Bourbon, finest there is, burned like a poker when Calhoun poured in into the bullet hole, but McMurray never felt a thing. "Guess it's a good thing you're not awake, eh?"

It took another several minutes to make up a clean bandage and get it secured before he started figuring out how to get the injured man and the prisoner on their horses and back to Aurora. "This isn't gonna be a nice ride, boys," he muttered. "I ain't gonna take a piece of crap from you, Olsen. One stupid move and you'll make the ride across the saddle, dead."

He poured the last of the coffee in a tin cup he found, stomped out the fire and worked to get McMurray on his feet. "What, what," Angus stammered, trying to fight off Slim.

"Easy there, Angus, it's me. Got your wound cleaned up and it's time we headed back to town. I need you to be just as tough and mean as you've ever been in your life. We've let most of the day get away from us and we got a long way to go."

"I'm sorry I passed out, Slim. I tried not to. I really did."

"I'm sure you did, Angus. Everything's fine except for a couple of things. You and Pete. How the hell am I gonna get you two back to town?" He knew the easy way was to kill Olsen and use all his energy to keep McMurray alive but that isn't the way of a U.S. Deputy Marshal.

"If I can get you on your horse will you be able to stay there? You've lost a lot of blood and I don't want you fallin' off that critter. I'm gonna tie our young and soon to be hung deputy city marshal tight to his horse. I don't want to have to tie you off, too."

McMurray was chuckling softly listening to Calhoun carry on and said he thought he'd be able to ride fine. "Get me some water, Slim." He was sitting with his back to a large rock, flexed his hands, rolled his head back and forth, and found that he could even smile just a bit. "I'll be fine. That damn leg does hurt a bit, though."

"We've lost a lot of this day, Angus, but I want to do everything we can to get back to town fast. I want to bring Olsen in alive and I know he'll spend every minute trying to get away from us. I'm gonna need you, Angus."

"I know you will, and I know I'm busted up bad, Slim. I want to say you can count on me, but what I have to say is, I'll do my best."

"Couldn't ask for more than that." He found canteens, gave one to Angus and took the other down to the creek to fill and tied it to his saddle horn. He untied Olsen's feet and got him in the saddle. With his hands cuffed behind his back, Slim tied Olsen's feet together from under the horse. Olsen's horse was tied tight to a tree and Calhoun walked back to get McMurray. "You just kinda sit there, Mr. Olsen. I do so much want to shoot you.

"All right old man, your turn," he laughed. It wasn't as hard as he thought it would be. Angus was strong as any ox in his stables and they got him in the saddle quickly. "You keep an eye on that wound, Angus. If it starts bleeding again, we'll stop and get you fixed up.

"If that young fool riding next to you even scowls funny, shoot him. Don't wait for me to say anything. Shoot him."

"My pleasure, Slim. Would you look at that?" He was pointing off across the meadow to a large elk bull and three beautiful females behind him. "Now I am angry, Mr. Olsen. Instead of babysitting your sorry ass I should be drawing down on that beautiful bull. That's a winter's meat for me, Olsen.

"Can I just go ahead and shoot the bastard?"

Calhoun was laughing as he mounted his horse and got the three of them underway. "Maybe we'll come back when this is all over, Angus." The elk watched the three horses move slowly across that meadow and down the canyon that would lead them back to the trail to Aurora.

CHAPTER THIRTEEN

"I've talked to two men who are willing to do what we want, Silas. They want a lot of money."

"No, Harrison, it would be better if we do it. Like you said, too many people already know about us. We don't need to bring in more. That new marshal isn't as sharp as he thinks he is and I've been watching every move he makes. He hasn't hired a deputy and he leaves that jail empty at night. Last night he left about six and went to the Borealis Hotel for supper and never went back to the jail until eight o'clock this morning."

"According to Henry the barber there were two fights at the Metropole Saloon that he didn't even respond to. It sounds to me that you have a plan, Silas."

The men were sitting on boxes in Houston's converted barn of a warehouse, drenched in worry. There were at least two men in this angry old mining town who could help lead them to prison, or worse, the gallows. Men were dead, federal agents were wounded, and an attack on government property had been planned by them.

"We not only have Childers and Throckmorton to worry about, Harrison, we have to be prepared for that damned marshal capturing Pete Olsen. That would be the end of us for absolute certain."

"Do you have some kind of plan, Silas?" He didn't mean to sound quick, but it did seem that Silas was evading his first question. "Have you ever killed a man? I think it would be best to hire a couple of men. We have to get rid of Brady Throckmorton as well, remember."

"Damn. It would be easy to slip into the jail and kill Childers. That's what I was talking about but Brady might be a little more difficult. Who were you talking with? Can we trust them? How much money do they want? What the hell happened to our plan, Wendell?" He was standing in front of Harrison, bristling with anger, and shaking his fist at thin air. "We had a plan and it was nothing like what we saw take place at that barn."

"Calm down, Silas. We'll work it out. Ezra Toledo worked for me at the mine and was caught high grading and chased off. He's got a temper, is big as a barn and according to more than one story has killed before. Just between us, he scares the hell out of me.

"Jerry Mace used to work for McMurray at the stables and was run off for being cruel to the animals. They are willing to kill for us if we pay them two hundred dollars each."

"That's a lot of money, Wendell." Silas Houston was shaking his head slowly, looking around the big area, slowly understanding that his world was coming to an end. He sat back down on the box and continued. "We'd be right back where we started. We'd have two men who knew what we did.

"What then, Harrison? Hire two more to kill them? And then two more, again, and again? No, we have to do this. Can you take out Brady Throckmorton? I'm sure I can kill Childers. Conrad Wilson wouldn't have any idea how to investigate a murder and we could simply take our time, clean up our business, and get out of town."

"I guess you're right, Silas. Let's do this together. Throckmorton lives in that men's boarding house near the Peabody Mill. If we catch him coming home we can lure him away and between us kill him."

"That's a good idea," Silas Houston said. "Okay, then. Tonight, after Wilson leaves the jail we'll sneak in and get rid of Childers, then go for Throckmorton. Let's meet at the Golden Globe for a beer about six and watch for Wilson to close up his office.

"We'll have to use knives, Harrison. Or clubs." Houston paced around the open space in his warehouse. "It would be better to shoot them but that would draw a crowd for sure. We have to be quiet." The worry about using a knife set in immediately and Houston had second, third, and fourth thoughts about what they were talking about. "I'm not sure I could use a knife on a man, Wendell."

Harrison had the same thoughts. "Let me have Toledo and Mace meet us at the Golden Globe and we'll make our plans from there. I can afford two hundred dollars, can you?"

"I don't want to, but yes. We should have the money with us." They left the old barn/warehouse separately, each with more anxiety and worry than when they arrived. A third person was seen to walk away from the barn ten minutes later.

"How ARE YOU FEELING, Charley? You shouldn't even be out of bed more or less running all over this fool town." Angie Whitaker pulled out a chair for the marshal and went for coffee. "Did you learn anything?" She put a cup down in front of him and laid a hand on his shoulder, squeezing gently. The café was empty in this slack period between the early breakfast crowd and the lunch crowd.

"Thank you. Your new city marshal is about two thirds stupid and the rest idiot. Where would I find the previous marshal? Ed Montgomery? He might know something."

"He's got a little cabin up Pine Creek a ways. Keep in mind he's the one that hired Pete Olsen and there are some in town think he was aware of or helped many of the outlaws in town."

"Yeah, I've heard that," Charley Green said with just a hint of a grin on his face. "That's why I want to talk with him. Slim gave me another name before they left. Do you know someone named Jacob Swarthmore?"

"Swampy? Sure, he swamps half a dozen saloons every night and sweeps the sidewalks in the morning. Town gives him a little shack of a place behind the jail, no, wait, that's Olsen's. Jacob's place is near Houston's barn. Just a lean-to. Why Jacob?"

"Slim said he seems to know a lot about what goes on in Aurora."

After a full meal and about a half pot of coffee, Charley Green headed up Pine Street, which became Pine Creek just out of town and found Ed Montgomery's little cabin.

Montgomery was sitting in a padded rocker on the front porch smoking a cigar. He didn't get up or even say anything when Green dismounted and walked through the gate toward the cabin. "Would you be Ed Montgomery, former Aurora City Marshal?"

"Who wants to know?" Montgomery almost snarled as he rocked back and forth slowly. His left hand held the cigar and Green saw that his right hand was very close to the handle of a large revolver on his hip.

"I'm Deputy U.S. Marshal Charley Green. Like to bend your ear some about that fracas that took place yesterday. Seems like your former deputy played a big part in it."

"Sure not surprised about that." He slowly got to his feet and opened the door to the cabin. "Come on in, Marshal and set a spell. Like a drink?"

"Thank you," Charley said walking into the tidy little cabin. The wood stove was hot and the two men sat down at what would be the kitchen table. Would be because the cabin just had the one room. There was a bed along one wall, a comfortable stuffed chair along another wall, the large table sort of in the middle of the room, and the stove along the third wall.

"What makes you think I might know something about that mess down at the livery?" Montgomery poured their coffee and produced a bottle of whiskey and two glasses.

"I was told that you came to Bull Morrison with some information about the robbery. I wasn't privy to that information and was knocked out in the fight. Slim said I should talk with you and somebody named Jacob Swarthmore. See if we can figure out who was behind that mess."

Montgomery laughed and slapped his open hand on the table. "I'll guarantee it wasn't Pete Olsen planned that heist. He couldn't plan taking a crap,

Marshal. This here mining camp is filled with vermin of the worst kind. You can hire a killer, a card shark, build a brothel and have it staffed simply by buying a cold beer or two.

"Now, about robbing a U.S. Mint shipment of gold protected by federal lawmen? That takes a bit of planning. None of the men involved in what you called a fracas yesterday has that kind of mind. I would say the original plan was to hit the shipment on the road somewhere and somebody changed the plan."

"That's exactly what I've been led to believe," Charley said. "The man or men who made the original plan were not at the barn. I've been told that Olsen wasn't supposed to be there either. I need to find whoever made that original plan."

"It became almost common knowledge that a shipment to the mint was being planned because of one of the men that works for the express company. Old Ted Hickson always plays his hand close to the vest, but one of his clerks, Brady Throckmorton has a big mouth. You can bet that whoever made that original plan got his information from the clerk."

"Would he have been in on the planning? It seemed to me an inside job from the first. Where would I find this Brady Throckmorton?

"Because of something I was told, I'm sure Throckmorton was not a part of the gang nor was he in on the planning. He's a dolt. On the other hand, I'd bet a big hand that those that planned it got their information from him. He has a room at Alfie's Men's House by the Peabody Mill. Catch him at the express office too."

Charley took a taste of the whiskey, smiled knowing it was the good stuff, and took another. "Good whiskey, Mr. Montgomery, thank you. I think I'll take a ride down to the express office."

"Someone else you might want to talk to, Marshal. You already mentioned him. Jacob Swarthmore. He was always a step or two ahead of me when I was town marshal. He usually sleeps all day and works all night swamping out filthy saloons. Silas Houston owns a feed and ranch supply store in town and has a barn out a bit, which he uses for storage. Swampy's the one passed that information on to me about the possibility of the ambush on the road to Carson City.

"Swarthmore lives in a shack behind that barn. Good luck to you," Montgomery said, walking Green to the door. "Feel free to call on me anytime. I took a great dislike to that Bull Morrison you work for but on the other hand, you and that Slim Calhoun will always be welcome."

Green was still chuckling to himself as he stepped from his horse in front of the Sierra Express Company office. "I gotta remember to tell Bull," he snickered, walking into the office. He was also thinking that Bull should be in Carson City by now and hoped he would hurry back to Aurora.

CALHOUN HAD the lead rope from Olsen's horse wrapped tight on his saddle horn. It wasn't always the best practice but he wasn't going to take any chances on Olsen making a break for it. "We'll ride until it's too dark to see, boys. One mistake from you, Olsen, and your days are over."

Olsen was riding slightly behind and to his right while McMurray was riding behind. They were making slow time working their way down the steep and narrow canyon to the main trail back to Aurora. The creek was running full, sparkling its delight with every rock it broke over, willows grew thick along the banks, and cottonwood trees offered immense shade for their ride.

Other than the fact Calhoun was escorting an injured thief and murderer, and was hampered by a wounded guide, it would have been a very pleasant ride. "You feel the need to stop, Angus, just yell it out. It's gonna be a long and slow journey."

"I'm feeling better, Marshal. Mr. Olsen is working hard to get his hands free of those cuffs. Did you put 'em on tight?" Olsen growled at the comment and Calhoun snickered some.

"I might be able to give 'em another notch if he keeps it up. On the other hand, if he should get a hand free we could both shoot him. Save court costs and save us worrying so about gettin' him in jail. Sure would make our trip a bit faster. What do you say, Mr. Olsen? Making any progress, are you?"

"When I do," Olsen snarled, "you'll be the first to die."

"Oh, my. Tut tut, there. Threatening a federal officer? Should I whop this ungracious fool, Mr. McMurray?"

The laughter infuriated Olsen to the point that he did some serious damage to one of his wrists. "He's bleeding pretty heavy, Slim. I think we better stop. He might of tore open a vein or something."

"Looks like the trail widens just bit right down there, Angus. We'll pull up and take a look. On the other hand, if he bleeds to death, we won't have to waste any of our ammunition shooting him."

McMurray simply nodded while Olsen erupted in some serious language and Calhoun continued to chuckle. "I think he's cussing in three different languages." He pulled his horse up to a stand of willows, stepped down, and tied him off. Calhoun led Olsen's mount to other willows and tied him off. "Don't go anywhere, Olsen. I'll be right back."

He tied McMurray's horse off and was about to help the blacksmith out of the saddle when Olsen started screaming at his horse and kicking him as best he could with his tied off boots. Olsen's horse got in a panic, ripped itself loose from the willows and started off down the trail at a high lope.

Calhoun eased McMurray to the ground and raced to his horse and was on the chase that fast. Olsen continued his high-pitched scream, kicked constantly, and his horse was racing as fast as it could go down the narrow and rocky canyon, Calhoun just yards behind. A horse is a prey animal and is sure that everything it sees or hears is out to eat it raw. The screaming and panic from Olsen made that horse run for its life absolutely certain it was about to die.

Calhoun couldn't ride up alongside Olsen because of a rocky canyon wall on one side and willows and a creek on the other. Instead, he raced up just as close as he could and used his horse to nudge Olsen's horse.

Horses don't like other horses nudging them from behind and Olsen's started kicking out, throwing its running rhythm way off. Olsen's hands were cuffed behind him, his legs tied together under the horse, and he was dangerously close to coming out of the saddle, which would have slung him under the horse.

The lead rope, still tied to some torn out willow branches, was flying about and if that horse should step on the end of the rope, it might just go head over heels. Olsen was no longer screaming at the horse, he was screaming in fear. His horse was no longer fleeing in terror, he was kicking at a bothersome following horse. Calhoun pulled back some, still laughing at the scene in front of him, and watched Olsen's horse come to a halt, breathing heavy, still wanting to kick at something.

"I went to a carnival, a circus, once, Mr. Olsen. It was down in Sacramento, and they tied a monkey to a goat and turned that goat loose. Funniest thing I ever saw, that goat bucking and snorting, kicking and jumping, and that monkey just whipping back and forth. Well, I believe what I just saw with you and that flea infested nag of yours might have been a bit more fun to watch."

Olsen started screaming and kicking again, no words, just howling anger, and Calhoun held tight to the lead rope. His horse was too tired to respond and Calhoun finally pulled his revolver, cocked it, and pointed it at Olsen's head. The man quieted down immediately. "Good boy. You've about tested me, Olsen. You gotta know I very much want to shoot you. Now, we're gonna walk back to where we left McMurray, I'm gonna save your life by stopping that bleeding, and you're gonna keep your filthy mouth shut. Got it?"

Olsen never spoke a word the entire ten minutes it took to ride back to where McMurray was sprawled in the dirt waiting for them. "I see the fool's still alive, Marshal. Any good reason for that?"

"Not really," Calhoun quipped. It took some effort to get McMurray comfortable, get Olsen untied and off his horse before Calhoun could take a few seconds to think about what their situation was. "How you feelin', Angus?"

"My leg hurts but it ain't bleedin'. I tried to stand up and that didn't come out very good. Damn."

"Yup," Calhoun snorted. He walked through the willows to the creek and brought some rags with him.

"Guess all we can do is get Olsen's wounds cleaned up and keep moving."

There was some serious squalling getting the cuffs off Olsen's wounded wrists. Olsen wouldn't have been able to say which hurt the most, his broken arm or the rents in his wrists. Great gashes in skin and muscle and heavy bleeding were coupled with Olsen fighting off the painful moves. "You buck and snort one more time and I'm gonna knock you cold and finish the job." Calhoun wasn't trying to be funny but McMurray couldn't help laughing.

Both wrists were a bloody mess of torn and ripped skin and Calhoun was wondering how to restrain the man's hands and arms. "I can't put the cuffs back on," he muttered, wrapping the injuries as best he could. "The bleeding's stopped but if I take the rags off and put the cuffs on, it'll start right back up."

Calhoun stood up from his nursing and Olsen reared onto his back and kicked out with both boots, slamming Calhoun in the back. Calhoun hit the ground rolling, his revolver out and one shot rang out, slamming Olsen in the middle of his chest. "Anger simply isn't always the best answer to a man's problems, Mr. McMurray." Calhoun dusted himself off and gave Olsen's body a long sad look.

They were back on the trail within the hour, Olsen strapped across the saddle. "We will make a little better time, I think. I'd like to ride straight in, Angus, if you're up to it."

"I'll do my best, Slim. It actually feels better sitting in the saddle than it did sitting on the ground. You ride at your speed and I'll do what I can to keep up."

"I won't leave you," Calhoun said.

"I know."

CHAPTER FOURTEEN

"Looking for Brady Throckmorton," Charley Green said to the clerk behind the counter. "I'm Deputy U.S. Marshal Charley Green."

"I'm Throckmorton. You one of the marshals that almost lost all our gold?"

"You got a bad mouth, mister. There was no gold lost and it sure as hell wasn't yours. We need to talk somewhere private. Don't give me a reason to force the answers."

Brady Throckmorton always looked up to the gangster element but was never quite brave enough to become a part of it. Instead, he found he was good at finding information the outlaws wanted and needed but he had never had to answer to anyone wearing a badge. This was his first encounter with a U.S. Marshal and the fear began to creep up his back.

There were always stories about the marshals, how they always got their man, how they always got their answers, how men who made their life rough came out losers, physically as well as mentally. Throckmorton feared Olsen, Houston, and Harrison, and now was about to face his worst enemy, a U.S. Marshal. Slim Calhoun had told Charley Green many times, "It's the intimidation factor, Charley. Use it to your advantage."

"I need to let Mr. Hickson know," Throckmorton stammered, his attitude all but evaporated in the high mountain air. He turned to walk toward the back of the building and Green went right over the counter after him.

"I'll walk with you," he said. Only Green was smiling when they entered Hickson's office.

"What's this, now?" Hickson did not like to be interrupted, did not like people simply waltzing into his office, and in reality didn't much care for Brady Throckmorton or anyone else who worked for him. "This is my office, after all. A private office."

"I'm Deputy U.S. Marshal Charley Green. I need to speak alone with Throckmorton here and he said you needed to know."

"What do you want with Throckmorton?"

"That's my business. Where can he and I be alone for a few minutes?"

"He's on duty. He needs to be at that front desk. Talk to him after work." Hickson was getting riled as small-minded men often do when their limited authority is being challenged and Charley Green had seen it a hundred times.

He carried a sly grin along with his narrowed eyes when he said, "Okay, fine, Hickson." He turned to Throckmorton. "You're under arrest, Brady Throckmorton. Turn around and put your hands behind your back. We'll go to the jail and have our little conversation." He slipped a set of restraints on the man's wrists and spun him around.

"Well, now," Hickson was stammering, his anger gone, his attitude slipped away somewhere. "No, you can't do that. Brady, tell him anything he wants to know. Here, Marshal, sir, use my office to talk with my man. I'll slip out and take care of the front desk. No. Don't arrest him, I need him."

"Thank you. That's very generous of you," Green said. He was having a hard time holding in the snickers but let his voice drip with slimy gratitude. He unlocked the cuffs and watched Hickson scamper from the office, a dejected man.

"Sit down, Throckmorton. You are fully aware of the attempted robbery of the Carson Mint shipment and I'm sure you probably know that men died in the attempt. One of the men involved is in custody and another is being chased and will be in custody soon. The men that we know were involved were not intelligent enough to plan such a scheme.

"I believe there are men behind that plot who were not involved in the fracas, probably leading men in the community. You wouldn't know anything about that, would you?" Green had a genuine smile on his face, reached across Hickson's desk and took a cigar from the general manager's cigar box.

"I suppose you've heard some of the rumors about federal marshals and how they get the information, eh? Well, we don't really cut off a man's leg and eat it in front of him, but there are other ways of extracting information." Charley Green just loved telling that story. Sometimes the marshals would eat a man's horse. Sometimes it would be the man's children. "Better say something, mister."

Throckmorton's mouth got very dry. He tried to swallow and there wasn't anything there. He looked at every single square inch of the walls and ceiling in the office and never once laid those eyes on Marshal Green. He said nothing but his mind was reliving that day. When he heard the gunshots at the barn he knew something had gone wrong and somebody might come and ask him questions, because, yes, he did know who was behind the attempted robbery.

But not what actually happened. That wasn't the plan. Something went wrong and he hadn't heard from either Houston or Harrison since. "I don't know nothin'," he finally managed to say. "Why ask me? I'm just a clerk here."

Green enjoyed watching the man's eyes flick about,

looking at everything except him. Seeing him try to swallow, squirming in that old hardback chair. "Come now, Brady, it is all right to call you Brady?" He didn't wait for an answer. "Surely you have some idea of who might be behind all this? Men are dead, Brady. Somebody has to pay for that. Maybe you were one of those doing the planning. After all, you do work for the express company. Have all the information on shipments and cargo."

Brady's face had flattened out, all emotion drained. Even his eyes dulled as what Green said hit home, and Green knew he was about to get the answers he needed. Brady was stammering out noises that weren't really words or sentences. Finally he said, "No, I didn't do anything. No," he said several times.

He was saying no but Charley was hearing different. Charley heard Brady say no I didn't do the planning. "If you know who might have been behind this plot to steal gold from the government, I can make your life a little better, Brady." He saw a sparkle and then the eyes dulled right out again.

"I see," Green said, quietly. "I think I understand." He stood up from behind Hickson's desk and walked quickly toward the door hearing footsteps almost run from it. He had to chuckle walking back. "You were involved and you know if you start telling me all about it, the others will surely kill you."

He was standing over Throckmorton who was slouched in that old chair, almost whimpering. "Of course there is always that possibility. Then again, Brady, if you don't tell me you'll be arrested and you'll hang right alongside Olsen and Childers." He stopped talking at that point and just let his words slowly spread their truth through Throckmorton's mind.

Green suddenly sat upright and leaned forward, looming at Throckmorton from across the desk. "If you do tell me who was behind all this you'll still be arrested, but if you testify against these vile criminals, you probably won't be hanged. You can make life a lot easier on yourself if you just give me an idea who was behind this plot."

"I won't be hanged?"

"Judges like it when a man takes responsibility for his actions, Brady. Tell the truth, let those who are guilty face the wrath of Lady Justice, and the judge will probably not hang you." Green stood up and took his big knife from his belt, tested it for sharpness, and grinned ever so slightly.

"If you don't tell me and I find out you do know, I'll spend the rest of my life seeing to it that you do hang." He spit those last words out, thumped the desk hard, and reached again for the restraints.

"It was Houston, Harrison, and Olsen. They were supposed to rob the wagon on the road. I don't know why they attacked the stables. That wasn't in the plan." Green could almost see a ton of guilty weight lifted from the man's shoulders as he spoke.

"I'm going to have to arrest you, Brady. You know

that. It is for the best anyway since those men will now be looking to kill you before you can testify. Tell me everything you know, including your part in the scheme."

It was an hour later that Charley Green escorted Brady Throckmorton down the street and into the city marshal's office. "Please hold this man for federal authorities, Mr. Wilson. There may be those looking to eliminate both my prisoners, sir. I've been led to believe you haven't hired a deputy yet.

"How do you plan on protecting these prisoners?"

"Why, they're locked up. In a cell."

"And you sleep at your desk, eat your meals at your desk? You are the saddest excuse for a lawman that I've ever encountered. Get this man locked up and I'm holding you responsible for their lives. I'll have your skinny ass behind those bars if anything happens to one of these men.

"By the way, I'll be bringing more prisoners in. I sent a messenger to bring a district judge to Aurora and he'll be here in three days. I also have arranged for the Justice of the Peace to hold an arraignment hearing tomorrow morning. Have these men ready before nine tomorrow morning."

Charley turned and headed for the door anger blazing in those deep eyes. "You may have won an election, Wilson. I doubt you'll win a second one. I doubt you'll make it through this term." What he wanted was a platter of steaks at Angie's café but what he knew he had to do was talk with Jacob Swarthmore, a man who lived in a lean-to shack and cleaned saloons all night.

HOUSTON WAS SITTING on a crate while Harrison was pacing around the old barn/warehouse. "You said they would be here, Wendell. If they can't be here to meet us we sure as hell can't be payin' them for something."

"Keep your braces fastened, Mr. Houston, we're right here," a voice said as two men walked in. "I'm Toledo, he's Mace." Ezra Toledo was tall and rail thin, hadn't shaved in several days, and his hair hadn't seen a brush in eons. Jerry Mace was short, squat, and filthy. "You got a plan for all this mayhem you won't do yourself?"

"You're working for me, you watch your mouth, mister." Silas Houston's anger boiled out of him at Toledo's attitude. "What makes you think you're good enough to do this job?"

"Whoever it is you want dead won't be the first man I've kilt," Toledo snarled. "Who is he and where is he? Do you want him hurt first?" Toledo was swaggering about, resting his hand on the butt of his revolver. He had his chin stuck well out from his scrawny neck and Harrison almost found himself chuckling at the sight.

"Yeah, a real bad man," Harrison said. "You're just a damned thief, Toledo, but we do want a couple of men dead and we are looking to pay you to do it. You ever killed a man, Mace?"

"Killed my pa when I was fourteen. He was tryin' to do my sister. Wasn't too hard to do. Reckon I can do another man just as easy. Besides, I sure could use two hunnert dollars right about now. Who are these men you want dead?"

Harrison spent the next half hour describing Throckmorton and where he lived and Childers and the jail. "If you leave now, you should find Throckmorton at that boarding house. Lure him out and kill him dead."

"I suppose you want some kind of proof." Toledo wouldn't let go of his attitude now that he felt he was a paid killer.

"You won't be paid until the town knows he's dead." Houston said. "The marshal leaves his office around six. Last night he left the front door unlocked, just walked off. Childers is in one of the cells."

"Well, that's it gents," Harrison said. "Two hundred dollars for each of you when we know they're dead. Don't let us down."

Toledo and Mace left in a hurry and Houston started pacing around the old barn. "What's wrong now?" Harrison asked.

"What do we do about them?"

CHARLEY GREEN WAS ABOUT to make his way

through weeds and brush toward a lean-to shack propped up near the back wall of an old barn when he spotted two men walking from the barn. He simply took a few more steps along the main street until the men turned away from him, then turned back toward Swarthmore's place. "Interesting way of life for this old man," he muttered.

It took some loud banging on old wood to finally get some response from inside the shack. "Who the hell are you?" Swarthmore said through sleepy eyes when he stumbled to his almost non-existent door. "You tryin' to tear my place apart?"

"Good evening, sir. I'm sorry to bother you, wake you up like this, but we need to talk. I'm U.S. Deputy Marshal Charley Green. Former city marshal Ed Montgomery suggested we talk."

"Marshal, eh? Got a lot of respect for you boys. That was a pretty good mess the other day," Swampy laughed. "I told old Ed that was gonna happen. Guess he told you boys. Come on in and make yourself comfortable." He ducked back inside the lean-to, holding the door open for Charley.

Green found himself inside an immaculately clean little room, lit with two candle lamps. There was a small wood stove, a bed, two chairs, and a small table. Two boxes piled on each other stood at the head of the bed and served as a table. "Like some coffee?"

"Thank you." Charley eased himself into one of the chairs and saw that inside each of the boxes by the bed were books, lots of them. "Quite a little library you have."

"My old law books. Used to be pretty good at what I did before me and old Johnny barleycorn got into it. Touch of brandy in this?" Swarthmore offered, holding a bottle.

"Thank you. I understand you overheard a conversation about the attack on our gold. We know the men we encountered certainly weren't those behind the original plot to steal the shipment, and those are the men I want." Charley green took a sip of the brandy and felt the burn all the way down.

"Now, that's fine brandy, Mr. Swarthmore. Fine indeed.

"Call me Swampy, Marshal." He took a sip of his coffee and got a little smile on his face. "You're sure right about Jake Jackson and that bunch of losers. They were plotting against Silas Houston and Wendell Harrison. Those two had brought Pete Olsen into the plan as well. Those are the three you want, Marshal."

The two men spent another half hour discussing the ins and outs of the law, the whereabouts of Houston and Harrison, and just how lovely Angie Whitaker really was. "It's a shame you had to give up your practice, Swampy. I bet you were a hell of lawyer."

"Can't fight what is, Marshal, but I was pretty good when I could stand tall. Haven't stood tall for some while now. Man's personal dignity is important,

Marshal, and I have found that I'm not much proud of myself. The women are always shouting about how bad demon rum and John Barleycorn are.

"Well, I just never did listen to 'em, I guess. Right now, Marshal, what you see is about the best I can be. You give 'em hell out there and don't take no horse dung from any of 'em. Good meeting a real man."

Charley left the little shack feeling a lot warmer than when he arrived and knew if he didn't get something to eat very soon he would simply lay down and go to sleep.

"That man does more than simply swamp the saloons, he lifts the best bottles of booze they have behind the bar." He chuckled to himself all the way down the street hoping he wouldn't slur his words when he ordered the biggest steak the Oriental Saloon and Chop House had.

"That old sun goes down earlier and earlier, Mr. McMurray. I'm afraid it'll be dark before we reach town. How you holding up?" They were riding on a well-defined wagon road in steep and rocky country. Slim Calhoun was leading Olsen's horse with Olsen's body slung across the saddle and tied off while McMurray rode alongside.

"No more bleeding that I can see, Slim. It hurts like the dickens, though. Probably got an infection going but I'll make it to town. We're not an hour out right now. I've been on this road many times and know right where we are."

"Good. We'll get this jasper taken care of, get your leg looked at by the doc and find a chunk of beef this big for supper." He held his hands out wide, laughing along with the blacksmith. Sure hope old Charley Green's feeling better. That bullet gave him a good whack."

The town was lit-up as usual, honkytonk music blasting from a dozen saloons, rowdy miners and ranchers wandering the streets looking for trouble, and brazen women standing in doorways with painted smiles of welcome as the three horses came down Pine Street. "Looks like a welcoming party," Calhoun chuckled.

"Like this every day, every night," McMurray said. "You learn to ignore it after a while. The doc's is right over there. You go on to the marshal's office, I can take care of things from here."

"What are you gonna do, crawl in? Hell, Angus, I got you shot, the least I can do is get you fixed up." It took some doing for Calhoun to get the heavy man out of the saddle and up the steps to the doctor's door. Doc Simpson let them in and got McMurray settled. Calhoun started back down the street, leading the two horses.

"Hey, Slim, hold up there," Charley Green hollered seeing Calhoun walking off. Calhoun pulled the two horses up and waited for Charley to get to him. "Looks like you had some trouble."

"Just got in. You look better. Help me with this and we'll have some supper. We need to talk some."

"You bet we do, Slim. You bet we do."

CHAPTER FIFTEEN

"THAT'S THE FLOP-HOUSE," TOLEDO SAID AS THE two men walked toward Alfie's Men's House. "You ever been inside? It's a filthy pigsty. Spent two nights there when I got to town."

"Nope." Mace said. "I know Brady. I'll go get him and bring him out to you. Keep your head on straight, Toledo. Use your knife and try not to let him howl or scream."

"I know what I'm doin'. He ain't gonna be my first kill." Toledo growled some and watched Mace walk up the steps to the boarding house. He walked around to the side of the building, in the shadows. It was late on a beautiful day, the sun would be down soon, which would have been better for their purpose. A light breeze danced through trees that were giving the impression they should start dropping their leaves.

High heavy clouds off to the north indicated the first storm of early fall just might be on its way.

Toledo pulled a large knife with an intricately carved handle and long broad blade. It was sharp as a scalpel and had a well-balanced feel to it. Ezra Toledo liked to tell people he killed a Mexican bandito and took the knife, but in reality, he found a drunk Mexican sleeping it off, whacked him with a shovel and took the knife. The only blood its tasted in the last two years was from a couple of deer he shot. He let his thumb ride across the edge of the beautiful knife and felt its keen sharpness.

He tensed at the feel of the blade and understood that he would be driving that knife deep into a man in the next few minutes. He was a braggart from the first word and only he understood that no man ever died at his hand. Blowing hot air at a saloon is one thing, driving a ten inch blade into a man is another. He sincerely hoped that Throckmorton wasn't home.

Mace walked into the open lounge area of the boarding house where a couple of tired looking mill workers were sipping on coffee, adding some whiskey to the cups between sips. "Lookin' for old Brady Throckmorton. Supposed to give him a message. Seen him around this evening?"

"Don't think he's come in yet. Me and Ed been here an hour or more and haven't seen Mr. Knows Everything About Everything." He laughed loud and poured both of them some more rot-gut. Have a drink?"

"No, thank you. Better keep looking for Brady. Tell him Jerry Mace is looking for him if he comes in."

The men nodded and Mace walked back out of Alfie's and down the steps. He found Toledo crouched in the shadows at the side of the building. "Hasn't come in," he said, chuckling at Toledo's attack stance. "Let's amble on down to the jail and take Mr. Childers to the promised land."

"Why do you always talk funny like that?"

Mace ignored the idiot and strode down the street. "We get Childers done then we can take our time finding Throckmorton. Quit playing with the knife. You're gonna hurt yourself."

Night came on fast as they walked toward the jail and with it all the turmoil of an active mining camp; Loud music from the saloons, boisterous activity on the streets, sidewalks, and in the businesses. The marshal's office and jail was dark and the door was unlocked when they got there.

"Light a lamp, Toledo. Too damn dark to move around in here. I think the cells are in the back there."

Toledo lit the lamp on the wall behind the marshal's desk, then found one they could carry and lit it. They walked to the door leading to the cells and it was locked with an old padlock. "Damn," Mace said. He took the lamp from Toledo and walked back to the desk. "Look for keys, probably on a ring. We'll need them to get into one of the cells too, probably."

"I WANT that steak real bad, Charley, but I saw a light on in the marshal's office riding in. Let's check on our prisoner, tell that fool Wilson that his deputy is dead, and then eat. All we had this morning was dried out biscuits and thin coffee. That marshal gives us any trouble we'll shoot him and cook him." Calhoun was laughing as they walked down the street.

"Yup, just like they say, we'll cut his arm off, make it into chops, and have us a fine supper."

"Sure glad you're feelin' better, Charley. Find out anything useful or have you just been hanging around with that pretty little girl from the café?"

"Both," Charley Green laughed. "Seems the man from the feed store, Silas Houston was behind the attempted holdup. They were supposed to hijack us on the road, not at the barn. He had a partner, one of the men from the mines named Wendell Harrison, and the two of them brought your buddy Pete Olsen in.

"Somehow the plan got all changed up, probably by one of the hired gunmen, and you know the rest."

"You've been a busy boy," Calhoun said. "Too early for Bull to be back, so it's just us, old man." They walked their horses up to the hitch rail in front of the jail and tied them off. "We'll leave old Pete out here for the time being. I guess Wilson will know where the undertaker would be."

"That door's ajar, Slim. We better be a little cautious here." The two men drew their weapons and slowly pushed the door open before moving quickly into the office. They were alone but saw the jail door open with the padlock hanging loosely from a nail.

"This ain't right," Slim whispered, motioning Charley to be quiet. Calhoun stood close to the jail door hoping to hear whoever might be in the back. He heard a boot thump the floor, threw the door open and lunged through, Charley Green right behind.

"Don't move," Calhoun thundered, his Colt cocked and ready. "Federal marshals. Don't move."

Jerry Mace was holding Childers' arms behind his back and Ezra Toledo had his knife close to Childers' throat, ready to slice it open. "Drop the knife, mister. Drop it now or die," Charley Green said, stepping forward and putting the barrel of his weapon on the back of Toledo's head. The knife clanked to the floor and Green smashed the gun across the outlaw's head sending him sprawling to the ground.

"Let him go," Calhoun said to Mace. "Nice and slow, now and you won't join your friend." Mace let go of Childers, spun and tried to knock Slim Calhoun out of the way but Slim saw it coming and met the charge with his left fist. "Outlaws are just born dumb, Charley," he grinned as Mace sat on the edge of the cell bed holding his broken and bleeding nose.

"Do you know these guys?"

"No, Slim, but I know how to find out." He stopped quickly and looked all around. "Where's the marshal? He's supposed to have a deputy on duty here." Charley Green was getting his anger up again.

"That bastard has made his last mistake." He looked around the jail, found Brady Throckmorton hiding under his cell bed and made sure he was unhurt.

"Wilson and I had it out while you were off galli-vanting about and I told him if anything happened to these men I was holding him responsible including jail time. He's one of the most arrogant bastards I've ever dealt with."

Calhoun was admiring Toledo's knife, testing its balance, and checking the edge. "This would have ended your life in a second or less, Mr. Childers. Looks like somebody doesn't want you talking to us. You know these idiots?"

Childers was white with fear, shaking, sweating, and whimpering all at the same time. He flopped down on the cot holding his head in both hands. He looked up as Calhoun asked the question. The thought of that knife being drawn across his neck almost paralyzed the man. Calhoun took a step toward him and asked again. "You know these men or not?"

"That one's called Mace. Jerry Mace." He was trying to get himself put together, took a long breath, and stared at Toledo. "I've seen the other one but don't know him. They were laughing about how easy they were making two hundred dollars each. Kill me and then Brady."

"Why is Brady Throckmorton in jail, Charley? He works for the express company doesn't he?"

"Yup, and for Silas Houston and company. He fed

them their information for the hijack. I locked him up to keep him safe. I'm gonna kick Wilson's butt from one end of Pine Street to the other. Damn."

Green grabbed Mace and shoved him into an empty cell after checking for other weapons, then got Toledo to his feet. "You're not half as hurt as you're gonna be, bad man," he laughed. "That rope gonna sting just a bit when it snaps your neck." He shoved him into another cell.

"Now, Mister Calhoun, sir. About that steak."

"I want to find that Wilson fool first, and we gotta get someone to stay here and watch these idiots."

Ira Benson from the Borealis Hotel stuck his head in the door. "What's going on? I saw the light on and the door standing open."

"Hello Ira," Calhoun said. "There's been a little trouble and we could sure use some help."

"I'll do whatever I can. Don't never pack no gun, though, and I'm too damn old to get in fights."

Charley Green chuckled. "Other than Pete Olsen, who did Ed Montgomery use as a deputy?"

"Swampy helped him a lot and that kid, Ted Foster, too. Olsen hated Foster and old Swampy mocked Olsen something fierce."

"I bet he did," Calhoun said. "Can you find Foster for me and get him over here? Then lead us to Wilson's house."

"The marshal's over at the Occidental Saloon, more 'n likely. He's a big shot over there. Young Ted's

across the street. I'll get him for you." Benson hurried
as best he could across the busy main street and into
the Borealis Hotel.

CITY MARSHAL CONRAD WILSON was at the bar
telling stories when Calhoun and Green came through
the swinging doors. They spotted him and walked up
to him, Calhoun on one side, Green on the other.
"Let's take a table, Wilson," Calhoun said.

Wilson could hear a threat and danger in
Calhoun's voice and didn't hesitate. The three took a
table away from the gaming and entertainment area of
the gaudy saloon. "My partner here wants to shoot you,
Mr. Wilson. I'm sorta thinking the same way. Deputy
U.S. Marshal Charley Green tells me you were going
to hire a deputy to keep our prisoners safe.

"Slip your mind did it?" He had spun his chair
around and was sitting on it backward as he glared at
Wilson. His arms were folded over the back of the
chair and he let his right hand slip down toward his
weapon. "What do you think, Charley?"

"Nope," Green said. "Shootin's too easy. I believe
it's a federal offense to willfully endanger federal prisoners, is it not?"

All Wilson wanted was a couple of years sitting
behind that marshal's desk and then make a run for the
Esmeralda County senate seat in the Nevada legisla-
ture. These men were going to deny him that and

maybe shoot him, too. "You don't understand," he sputtered. "That's why I'm here. I was trying to find someone to help me." Sweat was beaded on his forehead and his lips were quivering in fear.

"I'm sure you were," Calhoun said. "Another bottle and a few more stories and you might have made it, eh? Let's take a walk over to the jail, shall we?" He got up, put his hand on Wilson's shoulder and squeezed gently. "Up, fool, up," he snickered. Every eye in the saloon saw Wilson walk out the door between the two federal marshals and most noticed that Wilson's leather holster was empty.

Ira Benson was waiting for them when they walked in. "Montgomery will be here as quick as he can. I had to pound on the door. That man can sleep through buffalo stampedes I think."

"Thank you, Ira," Calhoun said. "Is Ted Foster in the back with the prisoners?"

"Yup, he is. He's mighty proud of that badge you pinned on him. He's a good lad and a hard worker." Benson pulled on his heavy coat and headed out the door. "Gonna be a storm before morning, I think."

Wilson walked around his desk and started to sit down. "No, no, no, Mr. Wilson. That ain't yours no more, no more," Slim said. "Let me have your badge, please. You are under arrest on federal charges. You'll be bunking with two men who we found inside your jail attempting to kill our prisoners.

"It's my guess they won't like you very much.

Won't like your arrogance. Won't like the fact that this was your jail. Yup, just won't like you."

"You can't do this. I'm the city marshal. This is my jail. You have no authority to arrest me or anyone else in this town. I'm the law in Aurora," he said, trying to stand as tall as Slim Calhoun.

"You're the south end of a horse going north," Charley Green said. He reached out and ripped the badge from Wilson's coat. "It would be fine with me to put him with Toledo and Mace, but I won't. You'll have your own cell, Wilson."

"Bull said he was sending a judge our way when he got to Carson City. I imagine he and judge will be here tomorrow or the next day."

"Not with this storm comin' in," Ed Montgomery said as he walked in the door. "Wind is coming up strong already. If the marshal is on the road, he's already in the middle of it." He shucked his coat and looked around the room. "What's this all about, Marshal? Ira Benson didn't tell me much."

"Take care of Wilson and then meet me over at the Borealis dining room, Charley. We can eat while we talk, Marshal Montgomery."

CHAPTER SIXTEEN

"It seems the later it gets the louder it gets around this town." Calhoun and Montgomery made their way through the crowded street to the hotel. "I know the mines are busy, there must be hundreds of men working under these streets, so who are all these people?"

"Believe it or not these men are the next shift getting ready to go to work," Montgomery laughed. "Don't know when they find time to sleep." He chuckled at his little joke. "Most are troublemakers, whether working at one of the mines, one of the ranches, or not working but coming up with the price for a bottle some way. Every confidence game you've ever encountered is being played at this moment somewhere in Aurora."

"Those are hard words, Mr. Montgomery but I

think I'm ready to believe you. What was it that put Wilson in office over you?"

Before the former city marshal could answer gunshots rang out and two men came racing toward them, one on each side of the street, shooting at each other. Montgomery and Calhoun hit the dirt and both had their weapons out and ready. "Stop!" Montgomery bellowed the word and surprisingly both men quit shooting but did not holster their guns.

Calhoun couldn't take his eyes off the scene in front of him. Two men standing across the street from each other, ready to kill and the former city marshal splashed in the mud attempting to get back on his feet, brandishing his revolver. It got surprisingly quiet. No gunshots. No expletives. Just the three men ready to kill.

"What the hell do you think you're doing?" Calhoun ripped the weapon from the man nearest to him while Montgomery disarmed the other. "You want to kill yourselves, get out of town to do it. How many people could have been killed or injured by this stupidity?" Calhoun smashed the man across the side of the head with his own pistol and kicked him is the butt as he fell down in the mud.

The other man was screaming that the man in the mud cheated him at the poker table with cards up his sleeve. "Go ahead, look," he demanded. The complainer was stocky, heavy chested, and carried a full red beard. "I don't abide cheats." Calhoun nodded and stooped down to pull the man's coat sleeves up. First the left and found nothing and then the right and found a pair of aces neatly tucked so they could be pulled easily.

"All right, friend, it looks like you're right. Ed, as the current city marshal is under arrest and in jail, and as Deputy U.S. Marshal, it is my pleasure to name you acting city marshal of Aurora. Please take this man into custody." Calhoun looked at the man who had been cheated. "How much did you lose?"

"About twenty bucks, marshal," he said.

Calhoun shook his head. "Twenty dollars and you were gonna kill for that?" He went through the muddy cheater's pockets and came up with more than two hundred dollars, pulled twenty, and handed it over. "Don't be runnin' through town shooting at people," he said with a scowl and sent the man off. "I still want that damn steak dinner and I mean right now."

"I just fined this boozer a hundred and eighty bucks for card cheating, Marshal," Montgomery said. "Let's go eat. Do you really have the authority to name me acting city marshal?"

"Probably not," Calhoun chuckled. "But in a town like this who's gonna complain?"

"You really did that?" Charley Green was still laughing hearing how justice was dealt out in Aurora, Nevada. "The man held a pair of aces and lost his money, his weapon, and his dignity while sitting in a mud puddle on Pine Street."

The laughter at their table rang out through the busy restaurant. "Bull Morrison is gonna love that story." Green was chuckling still as he told Calhoun that Wilson was in a cell and that Ted Foster was sworn in and holding down the jail. "Do you have any kind of a plan, Slim?"

"There is something that's bothering me first, though. Ed, how is it that Wilson was able to get elected? He doesn't have a clue about being a lawman and you've got a lifetime of it."

Montgomery was able to dodge the question earlier because of the activity on the street and didn't want to answer it now. It was embarrassing, belittling, and made him feel like a fool to even have to contemplate an answer. He sat, mute for several seconds, wondering just how it really came to this. He looked at Slim Calhoun with the saddest eyes the deputy marshal had ever seen.

"I got tired and sloppy, Slim," he finally said. "Gave up is what I did and let things get out of control. Should never have hired Pete Olsen and then when I did, let him handle things. I deserved to lose," Montgomery said. He was more than dejected but was glad at the same time that he understood why he lost.

"As far as Wilson, he had the backing of a rough element on the one hand and leading businessmen on the other. Express wagons and banks in this area were hit often, Marshal, and some of the gangs were protected by some of the businesses. Old Silas Houston for instance, runs a gang that attacks supply wagons and their booty ends up on the shelves at Houston's businesses."

"You know this and yet the man is running free?"

"You gotta catch 'em, Marshal, either with the goods or by witness identification. Merchandise isn't easily identified and men in black with masks aren't either. The bank in Body has been hit at least three times by a gang that lives right here in town. Hickson's express wagons are hit regularly and more than one person believes someone in his employ sets up the hits."

"That would be Brady Throckmorton," Charley Green said. "Just arrested him, Slim. He fed all the information on our little job to Olsen and company."

"As far as I'm concerned, right now, Ed, you're the law in Aurora. If the town council or county commission doesn't like it, then I'll deputize you and you can work for us until we get this mess cleaned up. It's the three of us against a town full of outlaws, so at least the odds are in our favor," Calhoun laughed.

"Will there be a backlash from our arresting Wilson? Will someone else try to free or kill our prisoners?" Slim knew the odds were against them if a large crowd became unruly.

"It's hard to say what will kick off shenanigans in this town," Montgomery said. "They burned down one

of the mine's hoisting works one Fourth of July because
of a rumor that the mine didn't contribute to the
barbecue fund. I can't imagine an uprising over
Wilson, and at the same time I can't say there won't be
one." He had an ironic little grin as he said this.

Charley Green wagged his head, laughing.
"Plan, Slim?"

"Oh, yeah. Step on toes, I guess. We have known
people involved in the attempted hijack, so unless a riot
or something comes along, we'll take them down and
wait for Bull and the judge to arrive." He looked at
Green with an ironic and knowing grin. Yup, he still
hadn't laid out any kind of plan.

"Let's roust Mr. Houston first and put the fear of
Huntsville in him, then work on that feller Harrison.
Would anyone else have been involved, Ed?"

"No, I'm sure this was their play all the way.
Bringing in Pete Olsen is what doomed the plan. Olsen
is simply out of control at all times. I don't think
anyone else was involved. There might be some
growling over arresting Wilson but you can handle
that."

"Let's get some sleep, then. We'll meet right here at
six in the morning and take out our fine hardware
dealer."

"What about Olsen? He's still strapped to that old
horse out there," Green asked.

"I'll take care of it," Montgomery said.

"I WAS GONNA PACK up all those pieces of gold, sell my business, and head to New York," Silas Houston grumbled as he moved around the little home he owned behind his feed and mercantile store. "Now, I'm gonna run like a dirty cur dog. Toledo and Mace should have gotten word to me hours ago. I have to believe they failed.

"Everything we tried to do failed," he all but stormed. "I have to blame Pete Olsen for most of the problems, but certainly not all. I've got to get out of here this morning. I can't wait."

Houston was putting bare essentials together and planning to simply ride off early in the morning. He had a pack mule at the warehouse and would load it and be on the road. He had several thousand dollars, clothing and food in a small pack, and would head north and then to San Francisco. He was interrupted by loud pounding on his door.

"Wendell. Good God, man. You look terrible. Come in, come in."

Harrison was sweating profusely from his almost run up the street from the Borealis Hotel. The wind was blowing hard and the temperature had fallen well below the freezing mark. "Olsen's dead, both Brady and Childers are still alive, and Toledo and Mace are in jail. That marshal even arrested Conrad Wilson. We gotta get out of town, Silas."

"Calm down, Wendell. Here, have a drink." Houston handed a bottle of brandy to Harrison along with a glass. "Slow down and tell me what you know. I'm packed and ready to walk out the door."

"The marshal and Angus McMurray rode into town just after dark with Olsen's body splayed across the saddle. McMurray was wounded. Everything else is just hearsay, Silas, but I know for sure that Wilson, Toledo, and Mace are all in jail and Childers and Throckmorton are still alive." Harrison gulped half a glass of brandy, coughed a bit, and drank the rest.

"There are four men sitting in that jail that know everything there is to know about us, Silas. We gotta get out of here."

"They are all in that little jail, Wendell." Houston sat back at the table and poured the two of them more brandy. One could almost see the gears turning as he put the situation together in his businessman's mind.

"That marshal has been running after Olsen, he probably hasn't had time to question Childers. That's an old wooden building and would go up quickly." He had an ugly smile as he continued. "If everyone that knows about us should happen to die in a fire, we wouldn't have to run." They tapped glasses and drank their brandy with satisfied smiles. "In all of Aurora only you and I would know the real story and we sure as hell ain't gonna tell it."

Harrison poured another glassful of brandy, poured one for Houston, and plopped down in a wooden chair at the kitchen table. "My God, Silas. It isn't really light yet," he muttered. "Do you have any kerosene? That is the answer and we need to move as quickly as we can."

"Out back," Houston said, grabbing his glass of brandy and leading them out the back door and over to a shed that Houston referred to as his carriage house. "I have two gallons of lamp oil in one gallon tin cans. We'll need rags, too. Look in the buggy, there should be some, maybe an old coat we can rip up. Hurry."

Lamp oil by itself doesn't burn very well, but when it's soaked into something, it burns long and hot. Within minutes the two were walking toward the back of the jail. Houston carried the two cans of lamp oil and Harrison had an armload of rags. They spread them along the base of the building, in the tall, dry weeds and next to the old wood. Poured the entire two gallons of oil on the rags, and lit them.

"Go home Wendell and stay there. Don't respond to the fire call. I'll be at my place as well. It'll take a few minutes for the fire to get going good and we'll be long gone from the area."

CHAPTER SEVENTEEN

"Good morning, Swampy. You're running a little late today." Angie Whitaker had coffee boiling, rolls and bread in the oven and Jacob could smell a large pork roast in the oven for the day's customers. "With this storm boiling in I wanted to get an early start of some good food for my boys." She danced about some, watching everything that wasn't tied down blow across the streets.

"It's a cold wind, Angie. Wouldn't surprise me if we have a blanket of snow on the ground by noon. That wind had me almost running coming down from my shack." He settled down at one of the tables with a cup of fresh coffee. "You got time to have a little talk with me?"

He had the most serious look on his craggy old face that Angie Whitaker had ever seen. She pulled up a chair and sat down with the older man. "I will always have time to talk to you, Swampy. You've always been a true gentleman, sir, and I'll be honored to talk with you." Her smile sparkled and Swampy could almost feel surges of youth scamper about his old body.

"That marshal, Charley Green, came by yesterday and got me thinking about what I've done with my life, Angela. I was a good lawyer not too many years ago and let that demon rum ruin my life. He's an insidious bastard."

"Charley? No, Swampy, he's a good man."

Jacob Swarthmore had to laugh. "No, little darlin', I mean John Barleycorn, not Charley Green. No, ma'am, Charley helped me see things I haven't seen or thought of in several years. You own this building, don't you?"

She saw a seriousness in his face, heard it in his words, and wondered just where all this was coming from. Jacob Swarthmore, Swampy, was, in most people's eyes, the town drunk. She leaned forward, her elbows on the table, wanting to hear more from this man. "Yes, this one and the little shed next door, too. Why?"

"I want to talk to you about getting some space from you. I'm going back in business, but I don't have any money. What I can offer you is fine representation and consultation any time you need it. I could convert that shed to an office if we can reach an agreement."

All the time he was talking he could hear the wind howling its displeasure at the world, could feel the building actually shake some at the powerful gusts, and heard windows and doors rattling about.

Angie jumped from the table where they were talking and raced out the front of her Lucky Lady Café, screaming. Swampy sat with his back to the front of the café with a strange look on his face. "How could I have frightened her so?" he said. Then he understood what she was screaming.

"Fire! Fire!" Angie was standing on the boardwalk, her skirts whipping about in the freezing wind, screaming and pointing at clouds of black smoke pouring into the morning sky from behind the marshal's office. Angie was hysterical and Swarthmore grabbed her and tried to calm her down.

"I'll sound the alarm, Angie. Get more pots of coffee boiling, the fire boys are gonna need them." He ran down the street to where a large pole stood with a brass bell on top and started pulling the rope for the alarm. Clang, clang, clang, it went, sending a chill through everyone that heard it. There was nothing more frightening in a mining camp than fire and this fire had the incentive of forty mile an hour wind to egg it on.

Almost every building was made of wood, and little of that had been painted or treated in any way. One building on fire led to buildings on either side, and exponentially to every building in town. On this morning, the fire was erupting through the power of vicious winds whipping it into a fury. A maelstrom of flame and smoke, sparklers of flaming ash spread about, and puny little hoses pushing piddling streams of water seemed useless.

Within seconds people started coming onto the streets of Aurora, responding to the alarm. Fire companies reported to their barns and soon hose wagons were being pulled toward the jail by muscular young men in their finery, helmets in place, grim faces grunting at the labor. Bucket brigades were formed, hoses were laid, orders were given, and the fire chief, Ned Wakefield, already knew he had lost the battle. The wind gods were against him from the start.

Slim Calhoun sat bolt upright at the first clang of the alarm and stood at the window of his hotel room watching the scene develop below. Within less than a minute there was mayhem on the streets, and less than five minutes later the screaming began. Calhoun was dressed and pounding on Charley Green's hotel room in moments.

"Jail's on fire," he said. "Let's go." Charley heard the alarm, too and was dressed and ready. "We gotta get those men out of there."

There was chaos on the street when they ran from the hotel and crossed over. The door to the marshal's office was bolted from the inside and their pounding didn't bring any response from inside. Calhoun turned and yelled at a group of firefighters manning a pump.

"There are men trapped inside. We've got to get this door open." He remembered that the door was heavily timbered and had iron braces across the timbers. "Bring axes and get some way for these men to get out."

Young Ted Foster was inside the office, his head down on the desk. His job was guarding his four prisoners but since they were locked up, the big wooden door to the office was bolted tight, a little sleep wasn't out of line. It was the smell of smoke that awakened him or maybe it was the screaming of the men in the cells. He was on his feet and racing for the back of the building and ran into a wall of acrid black smoke that all but dropped him to his knees.

He stayed on his hands and knees and crawled slowly along the aisle way and toward the cells. He couldn't see a foot in front of him, could hear pitiful screaming and coughing from the cells, and found himself coughing harshly. "I'm coming, men. I'm coming," he croaked.

He felt the heat as he got closer to the first cell and the smoke burned his throat, made his eyes run so that he couldn't see. He pulled his bandanna up around his face but it didn't help a bit. The cells were lined up along the back wall of the building and the heat from the fire was devastating. The old wood had been standing in the weather for years and was more kindling than building.

The fire raged along that back wall, black smoke

poured into the cells, and Foster made one final effort to get his key into the lock of the first cell he came to. He noticed that the screaming had ended, and then smelled that horrible aroma of burning flesh. He felt the key fall from his hands as he tried to crawl away from the horror.

ONE OF THE firemen handed Calhoun a double bitted ax and he started in on the door, taking mighty swings and feeling the wood slowly chip away. "That door's made of three by twelves held in place with iron bands, Marshal. You can whack on that for an hour and you won't be inside."

"I know you're right," Slim huffed, "but we've got to get to those men. Is there any other way into this building?"

"I think it's already too late," the town's fire chief said. "The building is fully engulfed and we can't begin to slow this fire down. Our only job now is to try and save the town."

Everyone able-bodied, man, woman, and child, was out fighting the storm, fighting the fire, working to save something. Business men were working to protect their stores, women were trying to protect their homes and children, and the firefighters were fighting gale force freezing winds on one side and blazing buildings on the other.

The fire chief, Ned Wakefield pulled a third of the

men off the pump brakes and hoses and told them to rest, that this fire would be fought well into tomorrow or the next day. "Get some rest, eat as much as you can eat, and come back here in two hours." He was standing with Slim and Charley watching his men do the impossible.

"I'll send another third off the line when these men come back, and then again and again until we either win or lose." He got a contemplative look on his face before continuing. "One of the men told me something about the fire. Come with me and let's take a look."

He led the marshals around the block and up behind the jail. "That's the back wall of the jail. That little shack there is where Pete Olsen lived, but this is what I want you to see," he said and bent down close to the still burning jail wall. "See that ash? That isn't wood and it isn't weeds." The stench made Wakefield wretch and he doubled over. "There's more, but I can't stand this any longer."

The three men walked back from the building into cleaner air. "My man said there was a distinct odor of lamp oil when he first came back here. This fire was set deliberately, Marshal. Those men inside were murdered."

Slim Calhoun was calling himself every name in the book as he looked at Charley Green. "My fault, Charley. Those men are dead because I was too busy feeding my ugly mouth instead of arresting those two men."

"Hogwash, Slim. No one could have anticipated this kind of response. Now is the time to find them, though. They must believe that Childers and Throckmorton hadn't told us about their involvement. They feel safe right now."

"If Bull Morrison doesn't fire my butt, he has every right to. All right, then. The damage is done and I'm going to have to live with this forever. Let's go get the killers."

The fire was moving at the whim of nature and the fire boys couldn't even slow it down. The entire block in which the jail sat was involved now. Seven buildings, some of the outbuildings, engulfed in raging flames. Hoses were aimed at building down wind from there in an effort to slow the fire.

"Cisterns are getting empty, Chief," one of the pumper captains yelled. Chief Wakefield sent men to outlying cisterns in an effort to pump their waters into the closer ones. A rider was sent to Body to enlist help, the mines and mills closed and their men were manning hoses and pumper brakes. The effort to save Aurora was immense.

"My God, Wendell, what have we done?" Silas Houston was standing next to his old barn of a warehouse looking down the hill toward a furious inferno of flame and death. He could hear building crashing to the ground, could hear men howling orders and screaming their pain, and knew he alone was responsible. This was his idea.

"No one could possibly know that we were involved, Silas. This was just an accident brought on by bad weather. In fact, I think it would be best if we went back into town and joined a bucket brigade or helped those who are injured. Guilty men wouldn't do that, would they," Harrison said with a nasty snicker.

"No. No, Wendell, I'm going to pack a mule with what I can and ride out of town. I intended to kill Childers and Brady, but I had no intention of this level of devastation. I can't stay, can't take a chance that that marshal doesn't know or suspect. You would be wise to do the same."

"If Childers or Brady Throckmorton had said something to that marshal we would already be in irons, Silas. Think about it. The one marshal chased Olsen down and killed him while the other marshal stayed in town. If he knew anything he would have chased us down. No, we're safe as babes at mama's tit.

"I'm going down into the town and offer my services to Wakefield. You do as you wish, but it isn't necessary. We'll be safer here than anywhere." He left Silas Houston, mounted his horse and rode down toward the conflagration feeling almost righteous. Houston watched him go wondering if he was right, if maybe he could stay and continue running his business.

"This isn't ash," Ned Wakefield said, seeing the white flakes being blown about. "It's snowing!" He was almost dancing in his excitement, yelling "It's snowing!" Over and over. "Give it 'em, boys. Get those pumps screaming, we've got a chance now, More buckets, more effort, now, boys. Give it to 'em." Through heavy, acrid smoke and flame, more and more of those fighting fires felt the cold flakes and understood they might just win the fight.

Slim Calhoun and Charley Green were standing on the wooden sidewalk in front of Angie's Lucky Lady Café watching the jubilation spread among the firefighters. "We need to figure out how to get those two bastards that did this," Slim said. "You have a good handle on the town, Charley. Which one is closest and which one might actually be at home?"

"Harrison's cabin is owned by the mine he works for and is near the mill. Hard to say where he might be. Houston on the other hand has a home behind his emporium but also has a warehouse in an old barn on the edge of town. Either or both men could already be on the run."

"That fire was set to kill whoever was in those cells," Calhoun said. "That tells me that they believe no one talked. Setting the fire should make them feel safe. Let's mount up and ride to that barn of Houston's. If he was about to run, he'd want to take stuff with him."

"He kept horses and a mule at that warehouse.

Swampy Swarthmore lives in an old shack out behind the place, tucked into a grove of cottonwood trees. I spent several hours out there. I'd start there."

The ride out of town was through streets filled with people moving possessions from their homes, getting ready to flee Aurora if the fire couldn't be stopped. "Keep a close eye on these people, Charley. You know this Harrison feller, I don't. In fact, I've only seen Houston from a distance."

"Bull Morrison is due in sometime today with that district judge. He'll love this mess. That's the barn up on that rise to your right, Slim." They nudged their horses into a slow trot and rode up to the barn's big doors, which were closed. "Animals are either inside or gone, Slim."

They dismounted and tied off at the rack in front of the barn. "Let's be quiet and see what we can. Don't want to walk into waiting guns," Slim said, motioning the two around the side of the barn. The old building was weathered, the planks along the sides were dried and they could actually see into the darkness. Slim held up his hand and knelt down close. The wind whipped snow blasted the two men huddled along the wall of the barn.

"Listen, Charley," he said.

CHAPTER EIGHTEEN

JACOB SWARTHMORE WAS BLACK WITH WET ASH having been on a pumper's brakes for the last hour and the engine captain told him to go rest and be back in two hours. They pumped hard for fifteen minutes, then a second crew took over, and then they were back. The young bucks could handle two or more hours of that extreme work, but old Swampy was nursing five or more years of hard drinking along with fifty-five years or so of just plain old age.

"Thank you, Cappy," he wheezed and slowly made his way to Angie's café. Chief Wakefield watched him limp down the street thinking that so many people looked at the old man as simply another washed up old drunk. Wakefield knew better and wondered just how many of the young smart mouths could have spent most of the morning working a hand pumper as Swampy had.

"Help for this ancient wreck, ma'am?" Swarthmore tried to laugh and just coughed instead. "Every bone, muscle, cell, and nerve hurts right now," he said, letting her get him settled in a chair.

There was something very different about this man who swept sidewalks and cleaned saloons, she thought. He seemed to stand a little straighter, had far more self-confidence, and wasn't afraid of those around him. Dignity, that's what it was, but she had to chuckle, though looking at the filthy old man sitting at one of her tables.

"You're a mess, Swampy. Here," and she poured him some coffee. "Drink this and then we'll get you cleaned up. You must be starving. You're too old to be out there on those pumps. Besides, you're supposed to be a dignified attorney, remember?" They were both laughing watching the snow, now heavy and wet, being blown about.

"There were four bodies in the jail when they finally got inside. The word out on the street is that the fire was set intentionally," Swarthmore said. "Murder. Whoever is responsible is going to hang." He sat for a couple of moments in thought. He knew who was responsible. He knew who was behind the plans to hijack the gold wagon. He knew who the prisoners were.

"Where can I find Charley Green?" he asked.

"They left here more than an hour ago, Swampy.

Looked like they were riding toward Houston's old barn."

"Good," he said. He polished off another cup of coffee before Angie took him into the kitchen and pumped a basin full of water for him. Washed and dried, his hair still matted and filthy with ash, he settled down for a platter of roast pork, potatoes, and biscuits. "I know I want a piece of your pie, Angie, but I don't know where I'd put it."

He was having a good laugh, rubbing his full stomach when he saw Wendell Harrison walk by the window of the café, heading toward one of the bucket brigade captains. "My heavens, will you look at that," he almost whispered. "Have you seen Ed Montgomery anywhere this morning, Angie? I've got to find him right away."

"He has five men helping evacuate that block just south of Pine. The fire was threatening all those little miner's shacks there. What's wrong?"

"I'll tell you all about it when I get back, little darling," he said. He was in his blackened jacket and hat and out the door in a wink leaving the girl to wonder just what got into the man.

Swarthmore was energized and on a mission, got through the busy crowds, tangles of hoses, and milling gawkers as fast as he could, looking for the former city marshal. It took three stops before he located Montgomery.

"Ed," he hollered, getting the man's attention. "Ed, we gotta talk. Hurry now, hurry."

"What is it, Swampy? Easy now, old timer, what's got you riled?" Ed Montgomery, even in an emergency as devastating as this fire, was always slightly laid back. "Okay, now. Calm down and tell me."

Swarthmore was wheezing from a combination of exhaustion and anxiety, coupled with heavy smoke and ash, and finally just sat down in the mud. "Sit down, Ed. You gotta listen and listen hard."

Swampy took the next ten minutes to tell Montgomery about Houston and Harrison setting the fires, about the marshals being at Houston's warehouse, and about seeing Harrison at the fire line.

"Feels safe, does he? We'll see about that, Swampy. Marshal Calhoun made me acting city marshal, old man, and I just named you my special deputy. Let's go see what we can do about this, shall we?" Montgomery once again had a purpose. It had been a long time since he had these kinds of feelings about the law, about lawbreakers, and especially about cowardly killings of men who could not protect themselves.

Montgomery helped Swarthmore to his feet and the two made their way back into the inferno. "I'm going to enjoy this more than anything I've done in five years," Montgomery chuckled, whopping his sidekick across the shoulders. "If I don't kill him first, I know I'll be bringing him to the hangman."

"Is that smoke, Marshal?" District Judge Seth Williams was riding along with Bull Morrison, Jory Anderson, and Easy Eddie Martin on the return to Aurora. "That's more than a morning's cook fire."

The icy wind had been hampering their trip since early yesterday evening and now the wind brought along a heavy blanket of snow. Visibility wasn't very good but what the judge saw was black smoke boiling in the wind.

"It is that," Morrison growled. He had been watching the smoke for several minutes and was aware that the fire below it was growing. In his opinion they should have been in Aurora sometime yesterday and weren't because of Judge Williams and his slow, slow ways. "I'd say they have a serious problem in that town right now. With this wind there might not be a town by the time we finally get there. I'd bet money that Slim Calhoun is behind it, too," he laughed.

"Jory, ride on ahead and find out what the situation is. Slim is all but alone there. Ride back to us fast. Judge, we gotta quit messin' around, here. I've got a wounded deputy and my special deputy alone in that town full of outlaws. Let's move it."

He watched Jory Anderson ride off at a lope and managed to get the judge's horse into a slow trot. It was times like these that drove Bull Morrison nuts. His and the Marshal's Service had the primary task of protecting judges. Morrison always took pride in never having had a judge even slightly wounded, more or less dead or held captive.

But he also had the responsibility of protecting the public, his own men, and capturing and bringing to justice criminals. "There are times," he muttered, "when I'd just as soon let the judge fend for himself and take care of my people." He nudged his horse into a fast trot, forcing the judge to speed up some, too.

It was more than two hours before Jory returned to the group with some horrible news. "I ran into Ed Montgomery," he said. "The whole town appears to be on fire. We need to hurry, Bull."

"Keep up or not, judge. My men are in extreme danger. Tell us the whole story as we ride, Anderson." He kicked his horse into a nice ground eating long trot and it surprised him that Judge Williams did keep up, probably so he could hear what was happening in Aurora.

SLIM CALHOUN MOTIONED for Charley Green to stay a couple of yards behind him as he worked his way down the long outside wall of the old barn. The wind was howling and filled with heavy snow, making the job of being quiet rather easy. They were nearing the end that opened into a large fenced area, probably originally set up as a staging area for harnessing teams of horses and mules. Their eyes burned from the heavy smoke billowing up from the conflagration in town and wondered just how much of Aurora would be left at the end of the day.

Calhoun reached the corner of the building and knelt down on one knee to take a quick look around the corner. He quickly ducked back, motioned Charley up to him, and stood up. "Houston's got a horse saddled and is tying packs onto his mule," he whispered. "He hasn't heard or seen us." Calhoun pulled his revolver, motioned for Green to do the same, and stepped around the corner of the building.

"Goin' somewhere, killer?" Calhoun barked out the words stepping quickly into the shade of the barn. He had his pistol aimed at Houston's broad chest and the man stood stock-still, fear chilling his bones. He was holding a length of heavy rope in one hand and was holding a box of something in the other. "Step back from the mule. Nice and slow and you might live long enough to hang, dog."

Calhoun was sure that Bull Morrison would have shot the man where he stood. Slim also knew that he was using every ounce of strength he had to keep from shooting him. If there was one thing federal marshals all agreed on, the killer of a lawman needs to die on sight. It would be so easy to just put a little extra squeeze on that trigger. It was a terrible inner fight he was having and, although Houston didn't know it, Houston was winning.

Silas Houston took a slow step back from the mule, following the command, hesitated for half a second, and threw the heavy box at Calhoun. The large, squat man spun and took off at a hard run toward the other side of the barn. Calhoun fended off the box but it knocked him back some and his aim was off when he pulled off a quick shot.

The long strong deputy marshal was far faster than the store-keeper and ran him down within fifteen yards, tackling the man and smashing the gun-barrel across the back of Houston's head when they hit the ground." Damn fool. You didn't have to get hurt you know. Shoulda just shot you."

Charley Green, still somewhat hobbled by the gunshot wound in his leg, caught up shortly. "Looks like he brought his own rope, Slim. Should we tie him up or just go ahead and hang the bastard."

Houston came to as they finished tying the man off. "Nice of you to join us, Mr. Houston. As you know, I'm Deputy U.S. Marshal Slim Calhoun and this is my partner, Charley Green, also a U.S. Marshal. It is my duty to inform you that you are under arrest, to be charged with open murder of a law enforcement officer, and the open murder of three other people.

"We'll work on an assortment of other charges as the time allows," he snickered. "Get up."

With his hands tied behind his back and his head hurting like hell, Houston had a hard time getting up. "I didn't kill any lawman," he stammered.

"Yup, there's the next charge, Charley," Calhoun laughed. "He's a liar, too. Young Ted Foster was a fully deputized town marshal and faced an agonizing death at your hands." Just saying it made his blood boil and he fought off the urge to shoot the man on the spot.

Instead, he hustled the prisoner to where the horse and mule stood. "Maybe you're right, Charley. We could just hang him right here."

"That would be best. Don't have a jail to put him in, anyway." Green was laughing, pretending to throw a rope over the limb of a tree.

The two joshed back and forth all the time unpacking the mule and putting him in a corral. Finally they got around to putting Houston in the saddle of his horse for the ride into town.

"How much of a town are we gonna find, Charley? My God, that fire has spread. I hope this heavy snow will help the firefighters. Rain would be better, I think."

"The snow's sure to knock it down, Slim. You think Bull will be back today?"

They rode slowly down the sloping road into the heart of Aurora, and the chaos of a town on fire. Hundreds of people were walking and riding the other way, trying to get away from the devastation. Some managed to look at them, and the wonder of seeing Silas Houston tied up showed in their faces.

"They don't know you're a murdering sumbitch, Houston. Maybe I'll tell 'em. Maybe they'd rip you from my care and strip the meat right off your filthy bones if they knew you started this fire," Calhoun snarled. "It would be a whole lot easier to take care of you if you were dead." He looked over at Charley. "Where we gonna put the fool?"

"How about at Angus McMurray's?"

They rode to the stables, which were at the north end of town and was saved by the winds of fate from the flames of hell still ripping its way through the little mining camp, and found McMurray sitting in his chair, his wounded leg stretched out on another chair. "Sure glad you're feeling better," Slim said.

"Thank you for saving my life, Marshal. Looks like you have another prisoner. This one gonna shoot me too?" He was chuckling and pointed at the big stove, almost red-hot. "Coffee's hot and there's a bit of Kentucky in my desk drawer on the right side, sir.

"You just missed Jory Anderson. He said Bull Morrison and District Judge Seth Williams would be here in a couple of hours."

"Good to know that. That wind saved your barns, Angus, but not the town, I'm afraid. This man is responsible and we need to ask your help." Slim was pouring coffee and looking for the good bourbon all the time he was talking. "Can you watch him for us? We need to catch his partner."

"Silas is responsible for setting the fire? My God, what is going on? He's never been an upstanding citizen, and I know you thought he was in cahoots with Pete Olsen to steal that gold, but burning down the town? Why?"

"Those men that were in the jail, at least the three prisoners, could identify he and Wendell Harrison, so they used fire to kill." Calhoun spit the words out. "Don't know what's gonna happen when people find out. Could storm the place, Angus."

"I've got my shotgun and pistol. Now I'll have to keep me from shooting him." The snicker was echoed by Calhoun and Green.

CHAPTER NINETEEN

"I WISH THAT MARSHAL COULD HAVE STAYED WITH us, Ed," Swarthmore said as the two men walked through the melee of the disaster. "Wendell Harrison is a strong man and I'm not." They knew that Jory Anderson had to get word back to Bull Morrison and couldn't stay with them to take Harrison into custody.

"We'll take him, Swampy. I don't much care for that Bull Morrison but I'll sure be glad when he gets here." Ed Montgomery slowed down to step over a knot of hoses before continuing. "Keep in mind, my friend, that Harrison lit the fire that killed those four men. Young Ted Foster was one of them. Don't let Harrison's quick mouth beguile you."

"I'm an attorney, Ed. If anyone gets beguiled, it'll be Harrison." Swarthmore pointed at a line of men passing buckets back and forth, with the filled going one way, the empty going the other. "He should be in that mess over there. Think he'll run when he sees us? I ain't very fast, you know."

Montgomery was looking at a line of men, all dressed in winter clothing and drenched from handling buckets of water. It was a line of men in black and brown coats, soaking wet, and now somewhat covered in snow and ice. They all looked alike to the former marshal.

Montgomery had to laugh and pointed toward a man helping set up the brakes on a pumper. "There's chief Wakefield. We're about to get some needed help, my friend." Montgomery called the chief over and in quick order laid out the situation. "Swampy thinks he's somewhere on that long bucket brigade there," he finished.

"It's not important whether he's dead or alive, but it is important that we have him. Can you give us a man or two?"

"You've got me Ed," Ned Wakefield said. "Never did much care for that arrogant pup and if he started this mess I want him to pay. Those men were locked in their cells when that fire was set, and that jailer, young Ted Foster gave his life to try to save them. Yes sir, Ed, you've got me. Let's go find that bastard."

Ned Wakefield came out of the mines, was about average in height but was built like a stone fence. Wide and strong.

"We'll be glad to have you, Chief. Ed looked at Swampy and said, "He worked underground on double jack teams and single jack, could swing a four pound single jack hammer for ten hours and want to start a barroom brawl after shift just to loosen up." He chuckled some but knew he was telling the truth.

"Thank you," is all Montgomery could say to Wakefield. What the fire chief had said to him had him choked up a bit and Montgomery would be the first to tell you it wasn't all smoke and ash at fault. "By joining in the fire-fight, he's feeling pretty safe, but the man is obviously a coward and we must look for him to run."

"You're a little different today, Ed. I didn't support you in the election 'cuz I thought you'd just give up. I was wrong," Wakefield said.

"I think that's him off to our left, there. He's not passin' buckets, just loungin' up against that hitchin' post," Swarthmore said. He nodded toward Harrison instead of pointing. Even so, Montgomery saw that Harrison saw the three of them coming and bolted toward the Lucky Lady Café.

Montgomery was still quick and was on the chase immediately, Wakefield with him, stride for stride. Swampy was left to bring up the rear, slopping through the mud and ice. Harrison burst into the café, half filled with tired and grimy men just off the fire lines. He dashed into the kitchen where Angie was putting yet another large pot of coffee to boil.

"What the ..." she started to say when Harrison grabbed her and roughly pushed her out the back door of the two story building. He all but flung the tiny lady over his shoulder busting through the door. The fire and all the activity was to the south, being pushed away by gale force winds, and Harrison made for the next street over. He had no plan except to flee, and now had a hostage for protection.

Holding up in a building wasn't the answer, he knew, but a horse was. He dashed between buildings knowing there would be men racing behind him, looking desperately for a four-footed means of escape.

"IF ANYONE WILL KNOW what's going on, it would be Angie," Charley Green said as the two men left McMurray's livery. "I could use a cup of coffee without more Kentucky floating around."

"I do like that man's bourbon," Slim chuckled. "We'll check with her, and then let's try to find Ed Montgomery and enlist his help in finding Harrison. I would love to have Bull come riding into town to save our butts and we hand over our prisoners."

"He might just shoot you, you know," Charley laughed. They made their way through all the gawkers and firefighters sprawled out on the boardwalks resting, and were about half a block from Angie's café when they saw Montgomery and two men race into the café.

"That's interesting," Slim said. "We better get up there, pronto, Charley." The two ran hard the last hundred feet or so and pushed their way into the café. "Where'd they go?" Slim yelled and three or four men pointed toward the kitchen. The two raced through the crowd, pushing people aside and into an empty kitchen. "Back door," Slim yelled.

"I HOPE there's a hotel left. Sleepin' on the ground just isn't for me." District Judge Seth Williams had spent the entire three days complaining, first about having to trot his horse, then about sleeping on rocks, and mostly about the rough ways of Bull Morrison. "We should have brought a buggy and proper camping gear."

"Jory said the livery survived the fire so maybe you can sleep on nice soft straw, judge," Morrison snickered. They were less than ten minutes from town and could already see the devastation that awaited them.

"My God, Bull. Half the town is gone." Easy Eddie Martin didn't talk much and Bull considered this almost a profound statement.

"Let's ride to the livery and make that our headquarters. I liked that blacksmith and he'll surely have all the news we want." He again put the group into a fast trot and they rode up to the barns quickly.

"Mornin' Mr. McMurray," Morrison said. He stepped off his horse, took the reins of Judge Williams' horse, and led the two into the barn. "Looks like the goddess of dawn is under siege."

"Aye, it is that." McMurray's eyes were filled with tears, from the smoke and from the sight of his town in flames. Snow was now coming down hard, still being blown about by the gale winds, and he ushered the group into his warm office.

"What's this?" Morrison was standing near the stove looking at the corner of the room. "You holding prisoners now?"

"Ayup, I am," McMurray said. "Slim and Charley brought him to me just a while ago. He's Silas Houston, one of the men responsible for the fire out there."

"What'd you do to your leg?" Morrison walked over to Houston, then back to the fire. "Get kicked by one of your clients?"

"Sit down, Bull, and I'll bring you up to date on what's been going on. I assume you got the gold to Carson City without problems. We on the other hand have had many problems around here."

The stove fire was stirred more than twice, the coffee pot re-filled and emptied as Angus McMurray outlined what had been going on in Aurora since Bull left many days ago. "I doubt that the problems are over, either. When Slim and Charley left here, they were going to Angie's café and then were going on the hunt for Wendell Harrison."

"Three people locked in their cells and burned to death because of this piece of bull crap over their?" Morrison said, pointing at Houston. "And his partner is on the loose somewhere in this inferno? People died in this barn because of him, too?" He stormed out of his chair toward Houston but stopped just short of the man.

"He needs to hang from a tall tree," Jory Anderson said.

"And a short rope," quipped Easy Eddie.

They spent another half hour getting their gear put up, making sure the judge was well taken care of, and left Easy Eddie to help McMurray with anything that needed done around the stables. "We want that man at trial," Morrison growled. "We want this town to understand what happens to lawbreakers and murderers." Bull stopped short, thinking on his feet. "We don't want the town to know any of that until we're ready, though. This could start a damn serious riot."

Morrison and Jory Anderson left the barn for the short walk to Angie's café. "The problem with a case like this, Jory, is the outcome. We have one of the men responsible for five or more deaths but we can only hang him once."

Anderson had to chuckle at Morrison's so-called logic. "Looks like they've got something going on at the café, Bull. Quite a crowd lined up there."

"Probably Slim making out with that woman. You can bet he's at the bottom of it." They hurried their step some and found answers they didn't want to hear.

HARRISON HAD to fight off Angie's continued attempts to escape and finally bashed her head with his revolver. He half carried, half dragged her through another alley and onto a street that had several saddled horses standing at hitching rails and posts. He took the nearest one, Carried Angie up as he stepped into the saddle. She didn't weigh a hundred pounds. He had her laid across his front and put his heels to the horse. They were on the Lucky Boy Pass Road in seconds. The horse's owner was left in the street screaming obscenities.

"I've got to put miles between me and that town. The only reason those men were coming after me is because Silas Houston must have talked. That coward. Well, maybe they'll hang him, but they won't get that chance with me." He pushed the horse up the steep and rocky hillsides for as long as he dared.

There was a long and steep climb to the top of the pass and he had to walk the gasping horse. There's a vast difference between a town horse and a working ranch horse when it comes to traveling a long distance. "Can't kill him. I need him more than I need this woman," he muttered. When they got to the top, terrible winds were howling and driving heavy snow, he found a small grotto off the main road, and dumped Angie Whitaker's unconscious body into the rocks.

"It's all downhill from here," he chuckled, turning back to the main trail. "From here south to Mexico is open country, no towns, no mining camps, no nothing. Even the Mormons have pulled out of this desolate place. I'll find that southern trail that leads to

Santa Fe and be safe."

Harrison's knowledge of the country was limited to

saloon talk by drunks who had never been there, and thought he might be in Santa Fe in a couple of weeks. He found nothing in the saddlebags on the stolen horse, there was no bedroll tied to the back of the saddle, and all he had with him was his revolver and a belt knife. With the first blizzard of the season roiling through the area, Harrison was in dire straights and was just beginning to realize it.

CHAPTER TWENTY

SLIM CALHOUN WAS RACING THROUGH CROWDS OF people, many of them pointing the way for him, Charley Green unable to keep up but following none-the-less. One man waved at Slim and pointed between two buildings, and Calhoun sped down the alleyway coming out the other side and almost bumping into Ed Montgomery and Ned Wakefield.

"He stole a horse and headed out for the Lucky Boy Pass," Montgomery said. "He grabbed Miss Whitaker, Marshal." Montgomery was shaking his head in anger and frustration. "He just snatched her up like a sack of potatoes, Marshal."

"We can't chase him on foot. Those that can, meet me at Angus McMurray's stables and we'll form a posse for the chase. Make sure you have a bedroll, side-meat, trail biscuits, and a rifle with ammunition. This may be a long chase. Hurry," Calhoun said.

Slim knew that Montgomery and Wakefield would be in that posse and hoped others would join. "Charley, are you up to it? A bullet to the head and another to the leg tends to slow a man down."

"Don't you worry about me, Slim. It's your talking that's slowing us down."

They were chuckling and running as fast as Charley could run back to the stables when Bull Morrison and Jory Anderson came bursting out of an alley. Calhoun quickly brought Morrison up to date and the four headed for McMurray's. They were tightening the cinches when Wakefield and Montgomery rode in.

"Swampy wanted to come but we talked him out of it. Man's got some grit in those old bones," Montgomery said. "He's taking care of things at Angie's café."

The wind was swirling through the open doors of the barn bringing lots of snow with it. Outside, gusts estimated at fifty or so miles per hour carried heavy snow with them laying a blanket of white over the charred remains of several blocks of the mining camp and boomtown. It was the aroma of the fire that lingered along with the memories of what the town had looked like.

"There won't be much tracking," Bull Morrison said. "With this heavy snow the best we will be able to do is stay on the main road. One important thing to watch for is someone venturing off the road, maybe looking to hide out in some rocks or something. This man knows someone will be chasing him so an ambush is always possible."

The six-man posse rode out of the big barn, each man bundled up for the storm and hard ride into high mountains. They turned up Pine Street and made for the main road over Lucky Boy Pass. The wind had calmed considerably but the snow had increased as well. Visibility was limited and the higher into the mountains the men rode, the less it became.

"He can't be anymore than half an hour ahead of us, Slim, but I can't see track one," Bull Morrison said. "If he pulls off this road we won't know it."

"He ain't gonna, Marshal," Ed Montgomery said. "I know this road well and there ain't nowhere to pull off to. He's not an outdoorsman, and he's on a stolen horse with a hostage. He'll keep on the road."

Slim Calhoun remembered the map that Angus McMurray had drawn for them when they were going to use this road to haul the gold to Carson City. "When we get to the top of that long climb McMurray told us about, he'll surely let that horse blow some. That's where we'll need to watch for signs that he got off the trail."

"Also," Ned Wakefield cut in. "When we get to the bottom of the hills, down on the plains, the road takes a wye. The north branch goes to Nine Mile Ranch and the south heads through the desert toward the old Mormon Springs. He could go either way."

"The man can't have any provisions with him. He was on foot with a wildcat for a hostage when he stole that horse. He doesn't know it, but if he survives this ride it will be because we save him," Calhoun snickered. "Angie doesn't even have a coat on according to those people at the café. We need to catch them soon."

It was hard riding through the heavy snow, up the steep trail, and despite the urgency of the ride, Morrison knew better than to charge wildly ahead. "He's riding a stolen horse so he doesn't have anything with him except that woman. If he doesn't get out of these mountains before sunset he's gonna die. I'll bet he doesn't ever have a fire starter with him."

"It'd make our job easier," Slim Calhoun said, "but he'd be killing Angie too." And then he put into words what everyone was thinking. "That is, if he hasn't already."

The long ride up the steep hill toward Lucky Boy Pass was hard, the horses labored valiantly, but even in the good shape they were in, it was obvious they were having trouble. The wind was still strong at the higher elevations, the cold was intense, and the snow fell in torrents.

Corey Peak lies to their north, topping out at 10,520 feet above sea level and Powell Mountain to their south lifts its craggy peak to 8,527 feet. Lucky Boy Pass splits the two at 8,039 feet, which makes for bitter temperatures during blizzards. "We're prepared," Slim said. "He's not, and it won't take much to put him in a panic if he's not already there.

"That's what kills people in foul weather. Panic. He may simply discard Angie, but right now, both their lives are in serious danger."

Two feet of snow was already on the ground as they neared the summit of the pass and the horses were fagged. "We gotta let 'em rest, Bull," Montgomery said.

"I agree. Let's take ten, stretch our legs, and then push on. When we catch him, I get first shot."

That lightened spirits some and the men stepped from their saddles into the drifted snows. Slim Calhoun said, "Look," and pointed at something bright red sticking out of the snow, about fifty feet off the road. He handed the reins to Ed Montgomery and plowed through the snow to the marker.

The red was Angie's apron sticking out of the snow. He fell next to it and started digging and pushing snow off her. *My God,* he thought, *will she be alive? How could she be in this blizzard?* "It's Angie," he howled back at the posse. He had most of the snow pushed away and tried to cradle her in his arms.

"Oh, no," he moaned, knowing she was almost frozen solid. "Aw, Angie," and he held her tightly. "No, Bull Morrison, you do not get first shot. I do," he murmured, slowly getting to his feet. Holding her close.

"We'll cover her in snow and leave her by the side of the road," Calhoun said. "She'll be okay until we get back. Let's mark the spot well and cover her so the animals won't get her." The anger was deep in his soul by the time the job was done.

"What kind of animal would simply throw a woman off a horse in the middle of a blizzard and just ride off. Even the worst animal you can think of isn't that cruel. This man, Harrison, lit the fire that killed those four men in the jail and burned half of Aurora to the ground. Now, he has proven just how evil he is."

The horses were well rested by the time the six men rode off, leaving the frozen body of Angela Whitaker alongside the Lucky Boy Pass Road. "It will be steep going down the east side of this mountain," Montgomery said. We'll probably run out of snow by the time we reach the valley floor, but we're also running out of daylight."

"He's right," Calhoun said. "We've got to get much lower, where we can find wood for a good fire, before that sun goes down. Once it's down, the temperature will drop like a rock. I doubt Harrison is that much in front of us." He let that thought roam around for a minute or two, pushing his horse some.

"Bull, are you up to a hard ride? Remember Tejon Pass three years ago? Remember the Indian rustlers? Can you ride that hard again?"

"You damn right I remember. Let's ride, Calhoun. Green, you and the others ride till dark and make camp. Ride tomorrow morning and watch for our sign. Let's go, Slim, hell for leather, boy."

Both men were laughing, yowling, spurring their horses in a mad dash off Lucky Boy Pass. "They have always been little boys," Charley Green said. "Deadly little boys who always get their man. They chased a Mojave Indian renegade stage highwayman for three days and the man pleaded for his life when they caught him. He believed they were apparitions, that nobody could catch him. They were spirits," Green laughed.

"You can be bet Mr. Harrison will be pleading when they get him all catched up," Ed Montgomery said.

Calhoun took the lead, forcing his horse to surge through the deep snow and heavy drifts, Morrison just a step behind him. After the first half hour Bull took the lead and Calhoun let his horse follow. The snow was still coming down heavy and hard but within two hours they began to see remnants of Harrison's tracks. All through the night, they rode hard and knew they were within striking distance of their prey.

Two men in excellent physical condition riding exceptional horses through high mountains during a blizzard, and they could see what they were after. They eased up on their speed, and let the horses catch their breath.

HARRISON HAD BEEN on the bucket brigade some that morning, at least long enough to get soaked through. Rain, then snow, and buckets spilling all over was now ice freezing his clothing to his body. The wind had quit but the snow fell heavy and cold. He was on a horse that hadn't been ridden hard for years and was ready to give up. He was shaking hard from the cold, and was having trouble concentrating. The effects of cold and the strain from the terror of being caught were taking their toll. He hadn't eaten or taken a drink of water since sunrise.

There wasn't a single thought about burning the town down, about killing four men at the jail, or of abandoning Angie in a raging blizzard. His only thought was getting away, getting warm, staying alive.

"I gotta get out of this cold. Gotta get a fire. Can't feel my feet or my fingers. Damn you Houston. Damn you Olsen." He was ready to blame anyone but himself. His plan was the best, why wasn't it followed? His plan after the fiasco was best, why didn't Houston follow it?

"Why can't I find partners as smart as I?" He saw a stand of aspen off to his left with some pine and scrub cedar tucked into a rocky but level spot and turned his horse toward it. Just getting off the horse was hard. His feet were frozen, his hands were frozen, and he hadn't spent more than half an hour on horseback at one time in more than two years.

He could feel the fingers of death tighten on his throat as he stumbled through deep snow trying to find wood for a fire. His feet hurt to walk and he found he couldn't take hold of broken branches, couldn't hold on to them, couldn't drag them to an area near the rocks where he wanted to get out of the weather.

He found himself crying in pain and fear and couldn't stop. He was shaking so hard from the cold that he couldn't get inside his coat to where he knew there were matches. He wanted a drink. He forced himself to calm down, stop the panic, think. He said it aloud.

"Think!" He slowly sat down in a cleared area near a large rock outcrop, pulled his knife, and started slicing kindling from some cedar he dragged over. He also had some sage he'd ripped out of the ground knowing that would burn hot and fast. It took more than an hour, the sun was behind the mountain already, and the cold was fierce, by the time he had the slightest flickering of a fire.

He had no thoughts of being followed. Had no idea even where he was in relation to the summit behind him and valley below. His only thought was fire, big hot fire, and he threw several large sage branches on his meager kindling. Sparks flew up and he watched the flames grow big and hot. He added some broken aspen branches, and pine boughs, then more sage.

His face and hands hurt, felt like they were burning, as they thawed from the heat. He was too close, had to back off and didn't want to. He hadn't had a drink of water since early morning and had nothing to melt the snow and ice in, nor had he anything to drink it out of. The realization was slowly forming that he was going to die and probably would not be alive when the sun came up. The fear crept slowly from deep in him, erupting in anger and terror.

Always ready to blame anybody and everybody for his failings, never once accepting the responsibility of a situation, he started cussing and screaming his anger at Silas Houston, Pete Olsen, even Brady Throckmorton, one of the men he killed in the jail fire. He was exhausted from the race for freedom, from the bitter cold, and from the exertion of his anger, and fell to the ground, pounding the rocks in frustration. The warmth of the large fire and lack of food and water, coupled with exhaustion brought sleep. It was a deep and fitful sleep on the bare ground next to a blazing fire.

He was amazed at finding himself alive when he awakened next to the smoldering remains of his fire. His whole body ached, his head throbbed, he was more thirsty than he could remember, and was hungry enough to tackle a bear. It was hard to get the fire restarted. His hands wouldn't work, his feet didn't work, and his head continued to throb. Eventually he got the flames licking the sky and sat as near as he could.

He gathered up hands full of snow in frost-bit fingers and sucked on it for half an hour or more and slowly came to realize that if he could get off this mountain he might just live through all this. He could find food in the valley. Even a jackrabbit would be a banquet now.

He hadn't taken care of that poor horse when he stopped the night before and the horse was in dreadful condition. It spent the night saddled and bridled, pawing through frozen snow to find scant grass, and was beat down from the day's hard ride over the pass. Harrison had a hard time mounting but finally got on and rode back to the trail and headed down toward the valley, standing bright in dawn's light. "I'm still alive," he muttered. "I'll make Mexico."

CHAPTER TWENTY-ONE

"I SMELL SMOKE," BULL MORRISON SAID, PULLING his sweat-flecked horse to a stop. Calhoun and Morrison had not stopped or slowed down for the entire night, riding their horses just as hard and fast as the trail and the animals would allow. The night was bitter cold, probably five or ten degrees below zero and heavy amounts of snow continued to fall.

Both men were blanketed in snow and ice, their horses covered as well. "Can't see a damn thing, Bull, but it seems like the smoke is coming from over that way. Maybe down the trail a quarter mile or so. Sun will be up shortly, let's catch that bastard sleeping."

Coming down the trail at a fast trot, the snow covering any sound they might make, they spotted Harrison's track from when he came back onto the trail. "He lived through the night, dammit," Morrison said. "That horse is limping. Look how his one rear foot is dragging. Let's go," and he spurred his gelding into a half jump, half lope through drifts of heavy snow, Calhoun right on his tail. It had been such a cold night that ice never got a chance to cover the surfaces of the snow. It was soft, billowing about, and deep.

Harrison was hanging onto the saddle horn, couldn't feel his legs or feet, didn't know or care whether they were in the stirrups. He kicked, whipped, and screamed at the horse but the tired and forlorn beast wouldn't go any faster than a walk. "I've gotta get out of these mountains, gotta get into the valley. There's a ranch people talk about, fresh horses, like a stage stop, north of here. Nine Mile, that's it."

The trail made a long sweeping turn around a bulge in the mountainside and Harrison caught sight of two men actually galloping their horses toward him. They weren't a half-mile behind and the terror of the sight stopped him cold. He turned off the trail into a stand of mixed pine and aspen and almost fell off the horse.

He scrambled through the snow into a culvert and tried to burrow under sage and cedar. He watched in horror as the two men pulled up short at the sight of his horse pawing through the snow for grass. He tried three times before he was able to get his revolver out of its leather and found he couldn't cock the hammer back. There just wasn't any strength or feeling in his hands and fingers.

Morrison saw the standing horse first and pulled up short, pointing. Calhoun stopped alongside him. "In those rocks and that stand of pine, see? Prints leading over that little bluff. I'll go to the right, you go to the left." Calhoun was off his horse, rifle in hand and making his way through deep drifts, circling to the right and staying in trees and brush. He could see Morrison doing the same thing the other way.

These two lawmen had worked together on so many chases, brought so many men to justice, they didn't need to talk or even motion to one another. Slim Calhoun knew what Bull Morrison would do, and Bull knew what Slim would do. They had brought Indians, bank robbers, highwaymen, murderers, even clergymen to their ends so often a chase like this was simply a day's work.

Harrison was in agony as he forced his now almost black fingers to pull the hammer back on his sidearm. Frostbite so bad meat was pulling loose from bone, pain so severe he almost screamed, but the gun was cocked. He watched one of the men move off the trail and into bushes and trees to his right and then lost sight of him. The other man moved to the other side.

"I'll get at least one of you," Harrison muttered. He pulled the pistol up and had to force his finger onto the trigger. There was no feeling at all. How was he going to aim and pull the trigger if he didn't even know if his finger was on the trigger? He was whimpering in pain, wanted to scream in terror, fear, knowing he couldn't defend himself. He knew it was Houston's fault, Olsen's fault.

Calhoun moved slowly through the snow, carefully avoiding small brush and trees so as not to knock snow off and giving his position away. He moved around a jumble of downed trees and rocks and saw Harrison not twenty feet in front of him. Harrison was looking around in a mad frenzy, waving his gun about, but not seeing Calhoun.

Slim saw Bull Morrison move through the snow to his right, knew the chief marshal saw him, and slowly moved closer to Harrison. Bull picked up a rock about the size of coffee cup and hurled it at the outlaw. Calhoun watched the rock arc toward Harrison and smack into the snow, missing the mark by less than an inch.

"Good throw," Calhoun muttered. Harrison jumped when the rock smacked next to him, the reflex firing the revolver. Calhoun watched the man, almost desperate now, try to re-cock the weapon. "Throw it down, Harrison. It's all over. Drop the weapon or die where you sit."

Wendell Harrison spun around and using both hands was able to get the hammer cocked but couldn't fire before Calhoun ran forward and smashed his rifle barrel across the man's head. "I'm gonna enjoy watching you hang, mister."

"He's a mess but I guess we have to try to bring him

in alive, Slim. Let's get a fire cooking and wait for Charley and the rest of them. Coulda shot him, ya know."

"You do surprise me from time to time, Bull." Calhoun pulled a blanket from his bedroll and wrapped Harrison's legs and feet in it. Another blanket was wrapped around his body with his arms crossed in front and tucked into his armpits.

"If we get him fairly close to the fire we might fight off the worst problems of frostbite. Maybe keep him alive for the hangman. Let's get some coffee boiling."

"About time you boys showed up," Bull Morrison said. He was sitting on a log in front of a raging fire eating some elk jerky he had softened in his coffee. Did anybody think to grab a bottle of that fine bourbon Angus McMurray keeps? Smoked elk puts a nice flavor to coffee, but it just ain't the same."

Slim and Bull had made up a fair camp, got a good fire going, and did what they could to keep Harrison alive. There was no way to tell how long it would take for the rest of the posse to catch up. They discussed heading back to meet with Ed Montgomery and the others but Harrison's condition and the pitiful condition of his horse ended the thought. Harrison needed to be wrapped in wool and near a fire and that horse needed rest.

"I suppose all this means you caught your man?" Charley Green slowly stepped off his horse, could hear the ice breaking from his greatcoat and pants as he did. "Rode him down, hunh?" He looked over to Ned Wakefield. You owe me a dollar Wakefield. You too, Ed Montgomery."

"What's that all about?"

"They bet me you'd kill the bastard, not bring him in alive."

"That was a fool's bet, Mr. Wakefield," Bull laughed. "It gives me great pleasure to watch a killer hang and no pleasure in killin' a man. Less of course I have to. But this one was a helpless pilgrim, all froze up, cryin' like a baby. Nope, not worth the price of a bullet. I hope they use cheap rope for the hangin'.'"

"Probably won't live long enough to hang, anyway." Slim Calhoun stepped out from behind a tree and waved to the new arrivals. "Frostbite is really bad and I'm sure gangrene will set in soon. We got at least a two day ride back to Aurora and I'm not sure that old stolen horse of his will make it."

"Slim always looks on the bright side of things," Morrison laughed. "Probably would have been best if I had shot the fool. Well, settle in boys, let's have something hot to eat then we'll start back."

Like all long distance rides, they could only go as fast as the slowest horse, and in this case that meant a long, slow ride. The stolen horse would not go any faster than a slow walk and nobody pushed him to. It was best to make a slow ride than have to double up for somebody to carry Wendell Harrison.

Harrison was in no condition to attempt an escape so he wasn't cuffed or even tied off, and Calhoun rode alongside the man to keep him from falling off. The blanket around his feet had been ripped in two and tied to them, and his hands were still wrapped around him. They were hours from the summit when they lost daylight and had to make camp.

"Will he make the night?" Ed Montgomery asked helping to get Harrison down from his horse. "I'm worried about what's going to happen when we get back to town. I'm sure the word has spread that we'll be bringing him back."

"Now that you bring it up," Bull Morrison said, "I'm worried about the judge and Jory Anderson. They're holding Silas Houston in the stables. Do you think the town will turn on them?"

"Sure as I'm sitting here, I do." Montgomery looked over to Ned Wakefield who nodded in agreement.

"The town burning is one thing," he said. "A lot of people lost a lot of stuff, valuables, but what will bring rage and danger is the four men who died in the jail. Particularly young Ted Foster. He kinda belonged to the town if that makes any sense and his death will bring a lot of anger to the surface."

"When they find out what this ass did to Angie, they'll be hard to hold back," Montgomery said.

"We'll ride long and hard tomorrow," Morrison said.

"Jory's a good marshal, Bull. He has Angus McMurray, and I'm sure he'll grab what help he can. We'll keep Harrison alive and ride hard." Calhoun poured more coffee, threw a chunk of elk in it, and pulled a blanket around his shoulders. "Night all."

CHAPTER TWENTY-TWO

THE FIRST RUMBLINGS OF DISCONTENT CAME when word spread that Wendell Harrison was responsible for the fire and had abducted Angela Whitaker. Anger slowly spread from saloon to saloon and more than one group was formed to take the situation in hand. It also soon became known that Harrison had a partner and that man was being held by federal marshals at McMurray's livery and stables.

"Silas Houston needs to die," a voice rang out at the Occidental Saloon. Twenty or so men raised their voices in agreement. Matthew Combs, a lead man at the Peabody Mill, and known highwayman, jumped up on a chair yelling at the top of voice, "Hang the bastard. He's the man that kilt Teddy Foster and them others in the jail. He burnt our town down."

Combs loved getting people riled but a thought came through that he might just be able to use a near riot to his benefit. The bank did not burn to the ground and with all the hullabaloo going on this might his big opportunity.

"We can't let those filthy dogs that kilt that Foster boy get away with it. We got to kill them," Combs howled to the delight of the crowd. "Silas Houston's been stealin' us blind for years, let's just tear him apart for what he done to our town. A man like that doesn't deserve to live."

The men were stomping their feet, shaking their fists in the air, screaming their anger, and Combs was plotting a bank robbery. "Let's go get 'em," he said, jumping down from the tabletop.

Ted Hickson had seen this kind of thing before and got out of the saloon as quick as he could, almost running to the livery stables. "There's gonna be trouble, Angus. They're gonna want to lynch Houston."

McMurray, Judge Williams, and Jory Anderson were having coffee in McMurray's office when Hickson burst in. "There's a bunch of 'em, Angus. And they're mean angry. They know you're holding Houston."

"I won't tolerate a lynching," Seth Williams said. "No sir, I won't."

"You might not have much say in it, Judge," Jory said. Anderson walked to the office door and called Easy Eddie and Jacob Swarthmore in. "We've got a problem about to start and I need help. A mob is forming to lynch old Mr. Houston and it's my responsibility to stop that from happening. It will get more than dangerous and you can bet bullets will be flying about."

"You've got me," Easy Eddie Martin said. "I know some of those men, I'm sure, and they'll be the ones that always start trouble. I've got my rifle, shotgun, and pistol at your service." He was so laid back, Swarthmore thought, that the word laconic fit him perfectly. He told himself to remember to ask him if he ever got excited or riled.

"I'm with you, Marshal," McMurray said. "At least most of me is. Can't move fast with this leg all bound up, but I'm a fine shot with my rifle and scattergun."

"Good. Let's find a good place to defend and get Houston moved." Houston was tied up and sitting on the floor in one of the corners. McMurray finally had to gag the man after listening to his constant complaints.

Jacob Swarthmore stepped to the stove to pour some coffee. "I've been half-way expecting this. Judge, I may not look like it, but I was a rather decent attorney up until just a few years ago and I can still speak well. Maybe between the two of us we can convince that mob to back off. Your authority, my jury pleading, and these fellers big guns might keep Mr. Houston alive for another day or two."

"You gentlemen take care of the prisoner and Mr. Swampy and I will do our best to keep the wolves at bay."

So, the grouchy old judge has a sense of humor after

all. Jory Anderson was chuckling softly as he hustled Houston to his feet and out the door.

COMBS HAD the crowd in a killing mood, screaming for blood, and filled with booze. This wasn't the time to let up and he kept up the harangue, citing each major building now in ashes, bringing up Foster's name often, calling their attention to the fact that "that beautiful Angie Whitaker was in Houston's partner's grasp. They burned our wonderful town, killed four helpless men locked in jail, and will take advantage of pretty little Angie."

That original group of twenty had swelled to near fifty by the time Combs stopped talking and they could smell blood. Two men came running into the saloon carrying a long rope already tied in a hangman's noose and the cry went up, "Hang the bastard," again and again.

The men followed Combs and the two with the rope out onto the muddy street, somewhat covered in filthy snow and ice. The stench from the fire was strong and that added to the frenzy. As they moved down the street, cussing and screaming for Houston's death, others joined, just as inebriated, just as filled with fury. They marched sloppily through the mud toward the stables, a mob in every sense of the word.

As they approached the barn Judge Williams and Jacob Swarthmore stepped out into the bright but icy sunshine. Judge Williams was an imposing figure, dressed in frontier canvas pants, white shirt, waistcoat, and full brimmed beaver hat. He had long wavy white hair tucked back over his shoulders, wore a full moustache, and a small goatee, also white as snow.

"That's far enough, men," he said. His voice was rich, deep, and flavored with a Virginia heritage. "There will be justice served, but it will be lawful justice." Jory Anderson carrying a double-barreled messenger's shotgun, his badge distinctively bright, stood next to the judge.

"Men," Williams boomed, "This town has suffered enough. Aurora doesn't need the stain of vigilante blood in its history. One man is in custody and another is being chased by federal marshals. I am here to see to it that these men get a fair trial before we hang them."

Jory Anderson had to hold back a chuckle at the way Williams said that. He had the shotgun at his waist aimed directly at Matt Combs, both hammers back and ready. McMurray was watching Houston and Fast Eddie was standing in the shadows of the barn doors, his rifle cocked and ready as well.

"He don't need no trial, Judge. All he needs is a strong rope around his neck." Combs yelled, turned to the crowd and raised his fist high. The crowd responded in voice but no one moved forward an inch. "Give him to us, we'll give him justice."

"No!" Williams boomed. "There is no need for any of you men to die. Your motives might be right, you believe what you've been told, but the law must be followed. The man may be guilty, but not until he's had a trial and found guilty will he be hanged." The judge's eyes were narrowed and that bright white moustache was bristling in the freezing air.

"We're living in a civilized society, men. We're not animals nor are we savages. Our lives are based on just laws, on honest judges, on fair penalties. Some of you men have wives and children who are generally safe because of those laws. If you so much as move forward an inch, many of you will die and justice will not be served. These men will be charged with crimes of the highest magnitude and if found guilty will hang." Jacob Swarthmore was no longer Swampy, the town drunk.

He was again the eloquent attorney pleading cases before informed juries, was standing as tall as he ever had, and there wasn't a quiver one in his deep baritone delivery. Seth Williams had half a smile as he watched and listened to this frontier attorney speak.

"Go home, protect what is left, help clean up this little mining camp, and let the law take care of these vicious criminals." Sweat was seen on William's brow, he was breathing hard, and as Jory Anderson watched, many in the mob were moving off slowly, some heading for home, others for the nearest unburned saloon.

"Go home," he said again, but softly, and turned to walk back to the barn. He took about three steps and turned. "The courthouse burned, so court will convene in this barn, day after tomorrow at ten o'clock sharp. A jury will be sworn in and Mr. Houston will stand trial, legally."

Jory hurried to the judge's side as they walked into the barn. "I have some pills in my little case, Marshal. Please get them for me." Anderson raced to the office and was back in a flash with a vial, found the judge sitting on a straw bale holding his head in his hands.

"It's my heart, Marshal. Doctors tell me not to get too excited," and he laughed gently, coughed a bit and reached for the vial of pills.

"Let me get you some water," Jory said, heading back to the office.

"No, but a good healthy dose of McMurray's bourbon will sure help." He took a couple of pills, chewed them up, and swallowed, grimacing just a little. "I'll be fine, Marshal. Do you think we stopped those men?"

"I know you and Swampy slowed them down, Judge. They won't attack as a mob. If anything, they may try to kill Houston tonight since we don't have a secure jail."

"I want that man as protected as it is possible, Marshal."

"He will be protected, Judge," is all Deputy U.S. Marshal Jory Anderson said, and the judge nodded his head understanding that the marshal would lay his life on the line to do the protecting.

"Swampy, you and me need to talk. Sit down here

with me for a spell." Two elderly gentlemen of the law were lost in their words for the rest of the day.

MORRISON PUSHED the group as hard as he dared in their drive to get back to the burned out Aurora. Harrison was unconscious most of the time and they finally had to tie him to the saddle. The old town horse was plowing through the deep snow, breathing so hard it sounded like coughing from someone suffering from the cons.

They stopped at the summit, found Angie's frozen body and tied her off on Slim Calhoun's big gelding. "I'll walk," Calhoun said. The sun was out and there was just the slightest breeze blowing from the north. More than three feet of snow had fallen in that brief storm and the temperature was near zero. They were at more than eight thousand feet above the sea, and within yards Slim felt perspiration on his forehead and biting cold on his cheeks.. He was thankful there was no crust of ice on top of the snow. At this altitude, the snow was soft and blew about with every step he took.

Charley Green and Ned Wakefield traded off leading the group through drifts as deep as six and seven feet, which tires a horse quickly. Bull Morrison was leading Harrison's tired old horse, and Slim brought up the rear, leading his horse. It was near sunset when they saw some dim light from the town, probably five miles down the road.

"I didn't think we'd make it," Bull muttered. "I was sure we'd have to camp one more night in this cold." Green stopped so everyone could catch up. "I can't tell if Harrison's alive or not, but let's not tarry. Mr. Green, ride on ahead and alert those at the stables that we're close. If there's trouble, get word back to us." Green was gone that fast, putting his horse into a trot, spraying snow in every direction.

"Mr. Wakefield, are you and your horse okay to lead us on in?"

"No problem, Marshal."

It was a very dark village they rode through, many building still smoldering, foul odors still in the air. A few buildings were lighted, a few people were on the streets, and the word spread quickly to the saloons that the posse was back. Wakefield led the group through the open doors of the barn and heard someone close them.

"Expecting trouble?" Bull Morrison stepped off his horse slowly, breaking ice as he did.

"Already had some," Swampy said, taking the reins for Harrison's horse. "He alive?"

"Maybe."

CHAPTER TWENTY-THREE

MATT COMBS WAS SITTING AT A TABLE WITH IKE Gillette, a down and out prospector who helped Combs with express wagon robberies, late night burglaries, and other schemes the mill worker might come up with. Gillette was small, stood about five six, weighed in at one twenty, but was fast on his feet if not his head.

"If we can keep these men riled, Ike, I got a plan that's gonna make us flush for a long time. That fire burned right up to the back of the Esmeralda Bank. We should be able to sneak in there late tonight. I've never seen Pinky Treadway lock the safe, have you?"

"You're right. He just pulls it to, locks the doors, and that it. He knows ain't nobody coming through those steel doors he had made. Think he'll have a guard or two? Wouldn't want to walk into a shotgun aimed at my head." Gillette was shot once in the back during a stage hold up that went bad and a few chunks of bird-shot still fester to the surface from time to time.

"I walked around the bank earlier and that back door ain't solid at all right now. I think a good kick will knock what's holding all to pieces. Looked like charcoal. Pinky's too tight to pay for a guard, and if he's guarding we'll just whack him a good one," Combs laughed. "Let's see if we can get these guys all stirred up, get them moving toward that barn of McMurray's, and we can hit the bank."

Gillette's eyes were the size of saucers as he thought about this idea. "I've always wanted to hit that bank, Matt but never said anything. Bank robbin' ain't the same as holding up an express wagon. I am ready for a pocket full of gold, my friend."

"You SEEM PRETTY sure of yourself that these fools are gonna try to kill Houston and Harrison tonight, Jory. Why is that?" Anderson, Bull Morrison, and Slim Calhoun were sitting at McMurray's desk having coffee and Kentucky. Charley Green was with Easy Eddie and prisoners while Swampy was still in discussion of the law with Judge Williams. "I thought you said that Swampy and the judge did a fine job dispersing that mob."

"They broke up just as easy as if he were lifting toast from the stove. That old drunk and Judge Williams had the crowd settled out in nothing flat. This feller Matthew Combs had 'em riled up good and then just let things settle down. Like he wanted that first attempt to fail. He was watching me and Easy Eddie, Bull, trying to figure out if there were more of us and where they might be. I'd bet he'll get another bunch drunk and frenzied before long."

"In my younger days," Bull Morrison said.

"Oh, no. Not another one of your long old stories, Bull," Slim Calhoun said. "This is serious stuff Jory's talking about."

"As I said," Bull huffed, "In my younger days I learned a great truth during a riot that took place along the embarcadero in San Francisco. An old Texas Ranger was with us and he said, 'watch for whoever might be leading. Betcha a double eagle he's got a motive.' Well, Slim Calhoun, you just think about that, old son.

"Does this Matthew Combs have a motive? Is he plannin' something that don't got nothin' to do with hanging our prisoners? Huh, Mr. Calhoun?" He sat back in and ancient rocker behind the desk smug as an old raccoon what just stole a chicken. "Well?"

"Them Texas Rangers were pretty smart, Bull. Yup, pretty smart." He paced around the office for a couple of minutes, poured some coffee and passed the pot around. "What do we know about this guy, Matthew Combs?" Calhoun loved it when Bull Morrison figured he got one over on him, but Bull wasn't aware of a conversation that Slim had with Swampy just an hour ago.

"Well, here's what I know about the fool. He's suspected of being a robber and thief, a burglar and confidence man. Stage coach drivers and messengers have all but called him by name on more than one robbery, he's been known to sell things recently stolen from homes in the area, and more than one holiday horse race has been won when the other horse all at once got leg cramps.

"Mr. Anderson is exactly right when he says Combs will lead another group to our fair livery some-time tonight and then disappear to do whatever his real plan is." Calhoun sat down in his chair and took a sip of coffee. It was his turn to have a bit of smug written bold across his face.

Bull Morrison snorted and poured some more Kentucky in his coffee cup. Slim noticed there was no coffee in the cup. "After a town has all but burned to the ground," he said, softly, "and one could get a mob all *serioused* up for a hanging, what would be vulner-able enough, or valuable enough, to go after. Certainly not some of the stores and businesses, not a saloon or hotel." He sat back in contemplation, just the hint of a smile spread across that mutilated face.

"About the only thing worth taking would be what-ever money might be kept in the bank I would say. Which, by the way, gives me an idea. Slim, old son, I'm really glad you told us about Mr. Combs. And Mr.

Anderson, I'm glad you are so sure that some kind of attempt will be made on our prisoners.

"Yes sir." Bull stood up and stretched. "Once again, U.S. Marshal Bull Morrison will ride to the rescue of those in need. Call in Montgomery, Green, and Swampy. We need to do some plottin' and plannin' of our own." He drained the coffee cup and headed out the back of the barn toward the necessary shack, chuckling to himself the whole way.

WHILE DAWN in the high mountains works its colorful way to an explosion of light, dusk seems to quickly snuff out all the light. In the valleys there might be glorious sunsets, but not in the craggy mountains. With Aurora's buildings still smoldering night came fast and there was little light from any buildings.

Ike Gillette started moving through the crowd at the Occidental Saloon, anger showing in every word spoken, talking about not waiting for some judge to probably let those two murderers of young Ted Foster off. "Those men can't be let go," he said over and over. "They need to see what real justice is. Hang them from the rafters of what's left of that old jail. Right over where they killed that poor young boy."

Gillette was a good speaker and his words were repeated from saloon to saloon all over what was left of Aurora, named for the ancient goddess of dawn. Matt Combs was in other saloons bringing up the fact that those dreadful men were also responsible for Angela Whitaker's death. "What do you suppose that vile Wendell Harrison did to that dear child before he killed her?"

Between the two of them, some fifty or sixty men were on the streets, with ax handles, ropes, rifles, and pistols about midnight. Combs and Gillette led them toward the livery and slowly melted back through the crowd, dropping out and making their way through darkened streets toward the back of the Esmeralda Bank.

"They'll light that old barn on fire sure as I'm talking to you, Ike." Matt Combs was beside himself thinking about how much money must be in the bank's safe. "There'll be thousands," he believed and said. "It's dark and cold, most people are exhausted from the day's activities so we shouldn't run into anyone."

They could hear all the noise of the mob as they made their way through mud, ashes, ice, and snow to the back door of the bank. It was burned but still seemed snug and didn't just fall open. Ike started working on the mechanism and within minutes had the door hanging loosely on its hinges. The old wood was singed enough that heavy pressure forced it to splinter.

"Quiet now," Combs said, stepping into the darkened back of the bank. "Through that door and to your right, Ike. The vault should be right there." Ike opened the door and froze stiff.

CHAPTER TWENTY-FOUR

"PLEASE, COME IN. BRING YOUR FRIEND." BULL Morrison stood just inside the door, his legs spread some, that monster double barreled shotgun of his at the ready, even with a grin on his normally angry face, inviting his flies to the web. Gillette stood mute, not quite understanding what was happening.

"Yes, please, go right on in," Slim Calhoun said. He stepped out of the shadows of the building and stood at the back door of the bank, his Army Colt in hand, cocked, and aimed at Combs' head. "Join your friend." He nudged the outlaw through the door and into the now well-lit bank. "Best idea you've had in a long time, Bull."

"Why thank you, Mr. Calhoun. We've got a nice little group of troublemakers here. Think Angus is going to be all right?"

Bull Morrison had sent Swampy Swarthmore to

find Pinky Treadway, general manager of the bank, to arrange for keeping the prisoners safe from the mob. Treadway had no problem turning the bank over to federal marshals. "Hell yes, you can keep 'em there as long as you're there with 'em," he said. "How safe is my bank with federal marshals spending the night there? You bet you can keep 'em there."

During the chaos of the town burning, people being kidnapped, murderers running loose, Treadway was sure the whole thing was a set-up for some group to rob his bank. He tried to hire extra guards but everyone was on the fire lines. This offer was a lifesaver as far as he was concerned.

As soon as it got dark enough they hustled Houston and Harrison by way of back streets to the bank and waited for what Calhoun was sure would be an attempted robbery. "Matt Combs, inciting a riot, attempted assault on a district judge, and attempted bank robbery," Calhoun said. It was very quiet in the marble floored bank as the charges were read out.

"Ike Gillette, inciting a riot and attempted bank robbery. In my opinion you two should hang right along with Silas Houston and Wendell Harrison, but of course, that will be up to the judge that you threatened, Combs. Whew, Bull, did you hear that? The man threatened the same judge that will pass sentence on his crimes. Damn fool, eh?"

Combs was in a rage and helpless at the same time.

Hands tied behind his back, feet tied together, and sitting on the floor listening to these yahoos make fun of him. The reality of the situation hadn't quite sunk in.

NED WAKEFIELD STAYED BEHIND at the livery to help McMurray if a mob did show up. "I see some torches down by the Borealis Hotel, Angus. Better get ready." The Borealis was badly burned in the fire and a group of men, maybe ten, were gathered there using boards and newel posts from the staircase for torches and weapons. "Looks like they're coming up the street now."

Angus McMurray was still hobbling on crutches and handed his shotgun to the fire chief. "You use this. I'd just knock myself down trying to balance on these sticks the doc gave me." The two were chuckling as they walked through the open doors of the barn and onto the darkened street to meet a subdued group of men.

"Ain't nobody here, boys. You're too late. Them marshals moved the prisoners earlier this evening."

"I don't believe you, McMurray. You're hidin' them murderers in that barn of yours."

"Why don't you take a walk through and check," McMurray snarled. "And when you come back you can apologize for calling me a liar." His right hand was no longer holding a crutch, rather, it was hovering mighty close to his pistol. "Don't much care for bein' called a liar, Gus."

Angus McMurray was held in the highest esteem by most of the people in Aurora and Gus Fletcher quickly stammered out an apology. McMurray's eyes had a nasty glint in the torch light, Fletcher was well aware of the man's shooting ability, and wasn't prepared to fight the blacksmith.

"You men have been all riled up by Matt Combs but have you noticed that slimy piece of hog crap ain't with you?" Ned Wakefield was ready to shoot the first person that made a move for the barn. "We've had just about enough killin' and burnin', men. Two men are in custody and a judge is here to see to it that justice is done. Put your torches down and go home. Sleep it off."

They watched as the group slowly broke off amidst quiet muttering and cleared the street. "Think it's over?" McMurray wasn't sure.

"I'd like to think so," Wakefield said. "I'm going down to the bank to let them know we're safe and so is your barn. See you in the morning." He walked Angus into his office and left the shotgun on the desk before heading for the bank.

"Remember, Ned, we got court in the morning. We'll have a town full of tired firefighters, hung over fools, and angry property owners. Think you could find some of your men to help set that up early in the morning?"

"No problem, Angus. See you then." It was a quick walk to the bank and Charley Green let the fire chief in the back door after making sure he was alone.

EXCEPT DURING MAJOR STORMS, sunrise in Aurora has always been filled with color and warmth in the rarefied air of the high desert mountains. Trees and bushes shimmered in the brilliant light and high clouds often went through the spectrum as the light bounced through their gauze. It wasn't to be on that morning.

Fires were still gasping for life, smoke billowed from many burnt out buildings, covering the little village. Two of the mines were shut down, their head frames charred remains of the conflagration. Luckily, the fires did not descend into the mines' depths and no lives were lost.

One thing remained the same for sunrise that day. Swampy was on the streets, but not to sweep the board-walks, but rather to gather help to turn McMurray's barn into a courtroom. He had tears rolling down his weathered old face as he walked past the Lucky Lady Café, dark and empty. "I'll miss you more than anyone I've ever known, pretty lady," he murmured. "You are the closest I've had to family in more than fifty years." He was leaning against the wall when Ned Wakefield came by.

"Mornin' Swampy. You headin' for the barn? Sure gonna miss Angie. More life in that girl than any others. I'm gonna grab a couple of men from the hose cart brigade and meet you at McMurray's."

Swampy nodded, wiped his nose and eyes, and trudged down the street, his mind wandering about some. One of the pleasures of walking the streets at sunrise, he said often, was being able to hold conversations with himself and not feel foolish when someone caught him talking to himself. He was a talkative old gent on his walk to the barn.

"Gonna have to make some changes, I guess. Can't have that shed next to Angie's café and that's for sure. I surely can't run an attorney's office from that lean-to shack of mine near Houston's barn. And I ain't gonna be the town drunk any more." There was a set to his jaw that hadn't been seen in more than five years.

He was interrupted by Ed Montgomery strolling down the street. "Things change and things stay the same, eh Swampy? Here we are, just like every sunrise, greeting the new day, but it ain't quiet the same, eh?"

"Good morning to you, Ed. I was just talking about that, myself. Gonna help set up the courtroom?"

"Yup. Had a long talk with that judge last night at the bank. He told me about your plans, Jacob. I couldn't be happier for you."

"Well, I'm afraid we'll have to make some adjustments on what I wanted. I was gonna rent that shed from Angie and turn it into my office. That ain't gonna happen."

"With a slight difference, it just might. I don't

think the county will let me stay on as marshal. Probably call a special election and I won't run. I think I'm gonna make a bid on Houston's feed and implement business and if I do, I'll rent out that little building to the side there to one Jacob Swarthmore, Esquire."

"Oh, my." Swampy had tears running down his face again, tried to wipe them away and just smeared ashes around, laughed at the attempt and stood stockstill. He looked deep into Montgomery's eyes and offered his hand. The two quietly set the bargain with strong hands gripped in trust. "Oh, my," Swampy said again, quietly.

JUDGE WILLIAMS RAN a tight court despite the fact this court was in a barn, which recently hosted an attempted hijacking of a major gold shipment and the death of several of those involved. "I'll not tolerate any outbursts from anyone," he said, his robes stained with ash from the fire.

"The County of Esmeralda has named Jacob Swarthmore as prosecutor and this court will now hear the charges." Swampy sat straight up, looking around in disbelief.

"I don't understand," he stammered.

Seth Williams chuckled and called him to his justput-together bench. "Mr. Swarthmore, when I was dispatched here from Carson City, the state's attorney general authorized me to name a prosecuting attorney for Aurora since the community did not have one.

"I had no idea that there even was an attorney in the old camp until you and I talked yesterday. So, sir, unless you have some objection, you are the city attorney for Aurora and since this court is convened to hear about the recent fracases, please present charges against the accused."

Swampy had a hard time keeping the smile off his face as he walked to the prosecutor's table and paged through papers the judge had already prepared for him. Tears, ashes, smiles, and hope spread through the old man's system and he had to clear his throat several times before he could begin.

"We'll start with the lesser crimes and work our way up," he said. "The prosecution calls first, Mr. Ike Gillette."

CHAPTER TWENTY-FIVE

THE TRIALS WERE QUICK. THE MARSHALS testified, the fire chief testified, some town folk testified, and the defense called no witnesses. Security was intense because of continued threats of ripping the men from custody and hanging them. Bull Morrison demanded that a public meeting be called and the town's council finally did so.

Morrison stood on a makeshift platform and thundered his anger at the people of Aurora. "The next person I hear threaten any of the men on trial will be arrested and charged with the highest possible crime. Just one more act of defiance of the law and I'm going clean this town up from north to south, east to west. I'm going to turn my deputies loose with orders to kill."

Despite the autumn cold Morrison was sweating profusely when he stepped down and did not have that ugly grin on his face. "After trial, I want you boys seen all over town, in every saloon, in every place where two or more people might congregate, and arrest anyone that even hints at a threat."

The four, Marshal Bull Morrison and his deputies were everywhere that night and many bartenders were heard to complain the next day. "Those marshals all but shut down my business. Men were afraid to talk, afraid to drink." One said. Morrison was in the Occidental Saloon when three men started badgering him about his protecting killers.

"One more word from any one of you," he said, quietly, leaning up against the bar, and you'll all be arrested. I protect the law and those men will get their trial."

It was an open challenge to three men who had spent the last few hours drinking and bragging and threatening. "You ain't gonna arrest all three of us," Spike Jensen said. He got right up in Morrison's face and spat out the words. The bartender had seen Bull Morrison in action just a few days prior and knew all hell was about to descend on his little saloon.

The glass full of rotgut whiskey flew into Jensen's face and eyes, was followed by a right body blow to the heart, and a knee to the groin. "You're right, I ain't gonna arrest all three of you." He looked at the other two men, his eyes burning with the thrill of a fight, that ugly scar turning bright purple, and stuck his chin out. "Unless of course these two are as stupid as you.

"What say you, gentlemen? Be nice boys or be

jailed jackasses. Your choice and you have three seconds to make up your mind." He let his right hand drop close to that big revolver he carried and glared at the two once belligerent men.

The saloon was quiet except for some sniveling coming from Mr. Jensen, the bartender could feel a killing coming on, and Jude Tyson went for his gun. It never cleared leather when a forty five caliber slug tore his heart to shreds. Morrison didn't take a chance on the third man and aimed at the middle of his head.

"No!" The man all but screamed, throwing his hands out from his body and lifted them high over his head.

"You men take care of the dead fool, you, help that idiot to his feet and march down the middle of the street to the courthouse." He made a big show of it and the word spread like the fires of hell through the town that the marshals would kill anyone who made any kind of threat.

JUDE TYSON and Jensen were held for trial, and the four others were found guilty of their crimes. Houston and Harrison were sentenced to hang while Combs was given life without parole and Gillette would spend ten years in the pokey. Swampy was elegant in his closing, citing law, quoting from history, and demanding justice. He laughed later saying he had been primed for about five years to use all those eloquent phrase but had not had the chance.

"They'll hang at sunrise, Judge," Bull Morrison said. When do you want to start back for Carson City?"

"Ten seconds after their necks snap, Bull. This is a depressing town, it smells bad, and I haven't had a decent meal since arriving. Take me home, Marshal."

They were sitting at a table in the Occidental Saloon munching on smoked elk, sliced cheese, and Dutch oven sourdough bread. "Were you and Charley able to find some clothes, Slim?" Jory Anderson had a slight grin on his face. The fire destroyed the rooms Green and Calhoun had at the Borealis Hotel.

"We'll be wearin' what we got on until we get back," Calhoun chuckled. "Five days so far and ain't been nobody fainted getting close to me. Houston's store is locked up until the sale, and it's the only store that carries men's clothing in the whole damn town."

"At least the town will get a fresh start after all this." City Attorney Jacob 'Swampy' Swarthmore said. "Courthouse is getting rebuilt, with a real jail made of stone and brick, not kindling, and we're getting a justice of the peace and city marshal in the election next week."

He got a contemplate look across his craggy old face. "I'm glad to say the Goddess of Dawn will brighten these old hills for a long time to come. Aurora has a new and fresh life ahead of her."

"I hope you're right, Swampy. You keep in close touch with me." Judge Williams was sipping at his coffee, laced liberally with brandy on this chilly morning. "My take on these mining camps is mostly negative, I'm afraid. Most have no other reason to exist than the mines. The ore goes, the town goes.

"Other communities survive because of diversification of resources. Farming and ranching, railroads, distribution of goods, and everything surrounding those enterprises that allows them to continue. I hope you're right, Swampy, but I don't think you are."

HANGING A MAN IS GRUESOME BUSINESS, and a public hanging is too often looked on as a celebration, a time for festivities of one kind and another, the entire community turning out to see that justice was done. There was pomp associated with a public hanging. It must be public, first of all, so the gallows was built right in the heart of the community and most businesses would be closed until after.

Aurora had one week to prepare for the gala celebration of two men being hung simultaneously. Ed Montgomery was still the acting city marshal and was not happy about being the hangman. "I tell you, Slim, the only time I've killed a man was when I was being threatened. I'm not protecting my life by pulling that lever and dropping those yahoos."

"Those men were a threat to the community, Ed.

That made them a threat to you. They wantonly burned alive four men and their fire destroyed many other lives. It's right that they hang and it's right that you pull the lever."

"It's gonna take half a bottle of Angus McMurray's good whiskey to get me to do it," Montgomery said. He wanted to chuckle but couldn't. "There's nothing more final, Slim. Silas Houston tried to commit suicide last night. I wanted to let him succeed so I wouldn't have to kill him.

"Where's the logic in that? I saved his life so I can kill him. Just like you did, Slim, when you saved Harrison's life up on the mountain. Saved him so I can kill him." Montgomery poured a healthy shot of whiskey and drank it right down, coughed some, and stared with dull eyes into the dust and dirt of the saloon. "I'm going to do it. It's my duty and my obligation, and, dammit, I know it's the right thing to do."

He sat quietly, tapped his fingers on the table, slowly wagged his head back and forth, and let the tears fall softly. "I've taken many men to the great unknown over the years by way of my weapons and never felt the least bit remorseful. Will I feel remorse when this is over?"

"I don't believe you will, Ed. You'll remember Ted Foster and Angie Whitaker and your jaw will tighten, and you'll not feel remorse. Conrad Wilson didn't have to die for being stupid, and Childers was a criminal, but they were murdered, burned alive in their cells. No, Ed, there'll be no remorse."

"I'm going to enjoy selling chicken food and single jack hammers, Slim."

Aurora lived up to its name on the morning of the hanging. The cold sky was brilliantly clear as the sun crested the eastern mountains and bathed the little mining camp with its warmth and light. Ed Montgomery had been up for hours, was dressed in his best pair of wool pants, white linen shirt, and heavy Mackinaw to ward off the cold. He did get a couple of cups of coffee down but wasn't about to try to eat breakfast.

"Good morning Slim, Charley. Thank you for being here with me. Where's Bull?"

"Bull's off being Bull somewhere. He's not one to attend such excitements as hangings. Strangest man I've ever known and I hope I get to work with him for the rest of my life." Slim Calhoun walked back into the vault area of the bank where the prisoners were being held.

Pinky Treadway was bank manager and jailer and wanted this hanging to get over with as soon as possible. "I'll have this bank open for business tomorrow morning," he murmured. "Five days we've been closed. I just hope my customers understand why I had to do this."

"Your contribution is duly noticed, Pinky,"

Calhoun chuckled. "Let's get these men on their feet." Calhoun pulled Wendell Harrison to his feet and Treadway put the iron cuffs on him. Montgomery stood near the door of the vault, that shotgun cradled comfortably ready.

"This way, Harrison," Montgomery said. "Just stand over there. "Okay, Slim." He watched Slim Calhoun get Houston up and cuffed, and they were ready for the long walk to the gallows, which sat prominently in the center of Pine Street. The sun had crested, the air was very cold, and the crowd was gathering.

"Can we expect any trouble?" Montgomery had been to hangings in Texas, New Mexico Territory, even California, and more than once there had been attempts at freeing those scheduled to die.

"Jory Anderson and Charley Green are watching the crowd, Ed, and you and I will be with the prisoners. Ned Wakefield has his fire boys scattered about as well. I'm pretty sure nobody will be trying to save these fools' asses. If there is trouble it will to do them in, and I don't think that's gonna happen."

At five minutes to eight the little procession moved onto the main street from the bank, walking down the middle of the muddy street toward the gallows, recently milled timber shining brightly in the morning sun. The wind kicked up, clouds could be seen in the far northern sky, and the threat of another storm was obvious.

To WALK two hundred feet isn't the least bit difficult unless you're staring at a gallows with two hangman's ropes visible, waiting for you. Silas Houston shivered in the cold as he stepped off the walk and into the street. Despite the freezing temperatures, sweat beaded on his forehead and with each step seemed to increase in volume.

He couldn't take his eyes off the gallows, the crowd already loud with their hoots and comments, and the fear searing through him, made him stumble. Nobody tried to catch him and he almost went down, which brought more hoots and foul comments.

"Hang the bastard," was the most often heard cry. "Hang 'em high." "Hang 'em twice each," some yelled. Slim Calhoun walked in front followed by Harrison, then Houston with Ed Montgomery and his shotgun bringing up the rear. Calhoun spotted Green standing on some rubble from the Borealis Hotel, and then found Anderson on the other side of the street, watching from the shadows of a building.

Judge Williams and Jacob Swarthmore were at the foot of the stairs leading up to the gallows platform. A representative of one of the churches stood with them and began reading from his bible as the men approached. Houston was crying softly as he mounted the steps while Harrison was almost belligerent in his attitude. It took a short prod from Montgomery to get

Harrison up the steps.

Calhoun stayed at the foot of the steps and watched Williams and Swampy follow Montgomery. The crowd was boisterous, angry, wanting revenge for what those men did to the men in the jail, to Angie Whitaker, and to their town. "I sure wish Bull was standing next to me," Calhoun whispered. If there was going to be trouble it would be in the next minute, from when Williams makes his statement until when Montgomery pulls the lever, dropping the two.

Williams thought the preacher was gonna talk for a month and finally shut him off. "All right, preacher, that's enough saving for today." He motioned to Montgomery who stepped forward and put a covering over Houston's head, then placed the noose just so. Williams then nodded to Harrison and Montgomery did the same.

"May God have mercy on your souls. I sure as hell don't," Williams said and nodded once again to Montgomery. There was just the slightest delay, and the Aurora acting City Marshal pulled the lever. Two trap doors flapped open, two bodies fell four feet before the rope snapped tight, and necks broke.

The crowd screamed their delight as the bodies jerked for a few seconds and then blew about in the frigid wind. It was eight oh five. Slim Calhoun turned from the crowd to help Williams and Swampy off the stairs, nodded to Montgomery, and escorted the judge out of the crowd.

"I want two good drinks of brandy and then let's get out of this place," Williams said. He had a sour look on his face and Calhoun remembered the stories Bull told about their ride down just a few days ago. Were they looking at an agonizing three days on the trail with this judge?

Bull Morrison came to the table, emerging from a noisy bunch of men, and sat down. "Just made a good deal, Calhoun. Bought us a back strap from a fine steer. Angus is cutting steaks right now. We're gonna eat good on the ride home. Those boys get sent to hell, Judge?"

"Let's ride," Williams said, standing up and heading for the door.

A LOOK AT NAME'S CORCORAN, TERRENCE CORCORAN (TERRENCE CORCORAN BOOK 1)

Terrence Corcoran carried a badge in Virginia City, Nevada until one day, in a drunken stupor, he shot the sheriff. Now he's returning to the Comstock looking to get his badge back and stumbles into a conspiracy that might put the sheriff, district attorney, and others in jail for a long time. A lovely working girl is brutally murdered, a Hungarian duke wants a Wells Fargo gold shipment, and the sheriff rehires him after first kicking him in a most tender spot. Corcoran was born on the ship bringing his family to this country, ran away to the frontier at an early age and brings his ideas of the old country and knowledge learned of the west to whatever mess he finds himself in. He's carried a badge, found himself in jail, and stands four-square for right, honor, and truth. You gotta love the guy.

AVAILABLE NOW ON AMAZON

ABOUT THE AUTHOR

Reno, Nevada novelist, Johnny Gunn, is retired from a long career in journalism. He has worked in print, broadcast, and Internet, including a stint as publisher and editor of the Virginia City Legend. These days, Gunn spends most of his time writing novel length fiction, concentrating on the western genre. Or, you can find him down by the Truckee River with a fly rod in hand.

Gunn and his wife, Patty, live on a small hobby farm about twenty miles north of Reno, sharing space with a couple of horses, some meat rabbits, a flock of chickens, and one crazy goat.

www.ingramcontent.com/pod-product-compliance
Lightning Source LLC
Chambersburg PA
CBHW021003260626
47169CB00006B/1919